I0621104

BLOODBAG

OF VAMPIRES AND MEN BOOK 0.5

KAILEY ALESSI

THE WHUMPY PRINTING PRESS

To Mom. Thank you for being such a fan of Tobias's story (even though you don't like all the swearing)

A NOTE FROM THE AUTHOR

This book contains dark themes including slavery, torture, physical and mental abuse, fire/burns, and religious tension. There is a scene of dubcon in chapter thirteen. Please proceed with caution.

The first twelve chapters of this book were originally published as a serial on Kindle Vella.

1

— · —

Tobias sighed as he locked up the shop, exhausted after spending most of the night struggling to keep up with orders for winter boot repairs. He pocketed the key and started down the street. There were still a couple hours until sunrise, and he planned to stop by the Temple of Clea for prayers and then the café to grab a quick bite.

The streets of Cesvic were busy with people preparing for the high holy days next week, when they would celebrate the longest night of the year. The moon was partially hidden behind wispy clouds, but the streetlights provided plenty of illumination, their orange glow flickering off the cobblestones.

The temple was only a ten-minute walk from Tobias's cobbler shop. He smiled when the spire came into view over the rooftops. Tobias's life was mundane—pretty boring, if he was being honest—but the temple always managed to cheer him up.

"People of Cesvic!" someone called.

Tobias's good mood instantly soured, and he rolled his eyes. *Not one of these nuts again.*

"The end is nigh! Lebne will return very soon to perfect his creation! You must prepare yourselves!" The man shouting was thin and short, with a flattened nose and a fevered gleam in his eyes.

Tobias was about to walk past when a hand shot out and grabbed his arm. He twirled with a snarl to meet the eyes of the zealot.

"You! Have you dedicated yourself to Lebne, to the Father?"

"No," Tobias said shortly, trying to shake him off. He was surprisingly strong for his size, and Tobias couldn't loosen his grip.

"You must, brother! You must prepare for the Father's return!"

"Let go of me." A current of unease gathered in Tobias's belly. "I've had a long night, and I'm really not in the mood for your ramblings."

The zealot's face darkened. "Ramblings? Oh, no . . . The words I speak are from the Father himself, the one and only god."

Tobias gritted his teeth. "I am a follower of Clea, and I don't appreciate your blasphemy."

The zealot released his arm in disgust and made a gesture to ward off evil. "Heretic," he hissed. "You worship death herself. The Father is merciful, but there are some things even he won't forgive."

Tobias turned without another word and walked away, fighting to keep his temper in check. His heart pounded as he ducked into the first alley he saw. He collapsed back against the stone wall and breathed in deep, trying to calm his racing heart.

The man was clearly crazy. But all the same . . . Tobias had heard rumors. Rumors about how just over the border, the Lucians were persecuting the followers of Clea. That they might soon ban the worship of her entirely. And while Cesvic was known for its tolerance, hostility was spreading even here.

Tobias clutched the sun pendant that hung at his chest under his shirt. He took one breath, then another. Then he stepped out of the alley and continued on until he reached the temple's marble steps. The ornate metal handle was cool in his hand as he opened the door and slipped inside.

The interior of the temple was lit by hundreds of candles befitting the goddess of fire. Tobias made his way toward the altar. The statue of Clea stood behind it, golden and majestic. There were only a couple other worshippers present. Tobias knelt.

I kneel before you, Goddess, in thanksgiving. The words of the prayer came easily, his lips moving silently.

Clea was the goddess of day, of fire, and of humans. She was the sister of Lebne, the god of night, of water, and of vampires.

Tobias didn't understand the people who were so vocal about Lebne being the one true god. The twin deities balanced each other. While Tobias felt closer to Clea, he still worshipped Lebne and had shrines to both gods at home.

Tobias sighed, closing his eyes. His run-in with that zealot had bothered him more than he'd thought. A wave of exhaustion rolled over him. He stood up, bowed to the altar, and left the temple. What he really needed was to eat and go to bed.

It was a short walk to the Crooked Vein, a café that sat on a quiet tree-lined street. The bell above the door chimed as he walked into the dim cozy interior peppered with plush sofas. Tobias breathed a sigh of relief.

"Why hello, stranger," Matthew said from his post at the front counter.

Tobias flashed him a smile. He had been visiting this café for years, and part of the reason was Matthew.

"How have things been?" Tobias asked.

"Can't complain. We got a new shipment in a couple days ago. Three new humans, and they are all very sweet. Would you like to try one of them?"

"Sure."

"Okay, I'll send you to Number 7."

Tobias nodded and headed to the designated alcove. Seated on the sofa within, knees pulled up to his chest, was a human.

Tobias sat down next to him. "Hello."

"Good evening, sir," the human said. His accent was Torin, and he couldn't have been older than twenty years. Tobias smelled a bit of fear on him, but overall, he appeared relatively calm.

That was another reason Tobias liked coming here. Matthew treated his humans decently, made sure they were given enough to eat and had comfortable beds and warm clothes. And he had a strict policy against abuse.

Tobias reached out and cupped his cheek. The human responded to the touch by exposing his scarred neck. Tobias leaned in and carefully pushed his fangs into the tender skin. The human relaxed in his arms as the venom took hold, and Tobias savored the hot rich blood that filled his mouth.

When he was satiated, Tobias gently lowered the human into a prone position so he would be comfortable while his body processed the venom. Then he got up, content and a bit sleepy, and headed to the front, where he handed Matthew a silver coin.

"You were right—he was really sweet. I'll see you next week." Tobias stepped out into the cool night air, licking the last bit of blood from his fangs.

2

—‧—

Tobias turned down the street and was only a couple minutes from home when the stench of smoke hit his nose. Along with it came the piercing sound of a woman's scream. Tobias didn't think as he ran toward the sounds of distress. He took a right and stopped dead in his tracks. The townhouse at the end of the row was smoldering, orange flames licking through the windows. Even where he stood, the heat blasted his face.

"My baby!" a woman screamed. "Someone save her!"

Two other women were trying to stop her from racing back into the flames. "You can't go back!" one of them shouted. "It's too dangerous!"

Tobias set his jaw and ran forward. "Where is she?" he asked the mother.

She snapped her head up to look at him. "Third floor, the first room on the left."

Tobias nodded and ran into the burning building, ignoring the shouts of warning behind him. Inside, flames licked up the walls. Tobias raced up the stairs. His lungs heaved with the effort as he climbed one flight, then another. The flames were even hotter on the third floor, and he held up a hand to shield his face. The smoke burned his eyes as he made his way to the first door.

He grabbed the metal doorknob and hissed when pain shot through his hand. His stomach dropped as he realized what that meant. Tobias steeled himself and opened the door, gritting his teeth at his stinging palm.

Flames filled the room, but they hadn't reached the far side yet.

Tobias spotted a little girl curled up the floor, her body shaking with sobs. He ran toward her, somehow not catching on fire.

"I've got you," he said as he picked her up. She couldn't have been older than three. She appeared unharmed, and Tobias hugged her to his chest as he raced out of the room.

The flames were spreading down the stairs now. Tobias used his arms to shield the girl as he ran down them. Distantly, he felt the flames lick at his legs. He was just starting down the final flight when he stumbled. He clutched the girl as he fell down the stairs, the impact driving the air from his lungs. The little girl screamed, and Tobias struggled to take in a breath. By sheer force of will, he got himself back up and staggered the rest of the way to the door. He burst out of the house, only then becoming aware of the tears running down his face.

"Cynthia!"

Tobias didn't protest as the woman rushed forward to take her child into her arms.

"Thank you, sir. Thank you," she said.

Tobias nodded as he put his hands to his knees, swaying a little. "Is there anyone else in the house?" he croaked, his throat sore.

"Just the blood bag," the woman said distractedly.

Tobias sucked in another deep breath. "Where are they?"

The woman looked up in surprise. "The third floor, but honestly, he isn't worth it."

Tobias hardly heard her; he was already running back toward the burning structure. He wasn't about to leave a human to burn to death.

The flames seemed even hotter when he burst through the entrance this time. He could hardly see through the flames and smoke but somehow managed to find his way to the rapidly burning stairs and started up them. He prayed they would still be usable when he came back down.

Tobias paused at the top of the stairs, heart pounding. The third floor was completely engulfed in flames. He had no idea where the human was.

"Where are you?" he yelled, his voice raw. He could hardly hear over the pounding of his heart, much less the crackling of the flames as they greedily devoured the timber holding the house up. He would have to check every room.

He opened the first door on the right only to be hit by a wall of flame. He stumbled back as the flames licked at his legs. He muffled a scream, then ran farther down the hallway.

"Blood bag!" he called desperately.

"Here!" The weak voice sounded like it was coming from the door on his left—the door that was currently falling off its hinges as it burned. Tobias shoved it aside and entered the room.

He couldn't see anything, the smoke and flames offering nothing but a wall of red, yellow, and gray.

"Where are you?" he called, his voice cracking.

There was no response.

The heat was so intense that it took all of Tobias's willpower not to retreat from the room. Instead, he made his way farther into the flames. They whipped around his legs, and he cried out, but then his eyes landed on a door near the back of the room. He stumbled toward it. The flames were less intense there, and when he reached his hand out, the doorknob was warm instead of scalding.

He opened the door and coughed as the smoke from inside filled his lungs. His vision blurred. If he didn't get out of here soon, he would die.

Inside the smoky closet, a figure huddled on the floor. Tobias crossed to it in two strides and crouched down. Tobias let out a string of curses when he saw the shackles around the human's wrists. The human hadn't even had a chance to escape on his own. When the human didn't move or speak, Tobias realized he was unconscious. Tobias looked around the room, but there was no key in sight.

"Hey." Tobias reached out to lightly slap the human's cheek.

The human groaned, slowly blinking his eyes open.

"Where's the key?" Tobias asked. The human only stared at him, his gaze unfocused, and Tobias was hit by a coughing fit. When he'd recovered, he shook the human's shoulders. "Tell me where the key to your shackles is. I need to get you out of here."

The human's head drooped. "Master h-has it," he said with a raspy voice.

Tobias cursed again. He examined the metal shackles. They were a bit loose, and the flames were starting to enter the room. Tobias pulled the human's left hand down sharply, hoping to get it out. The human cried out, but his hand stayed stuck.

The scent of blood wafted toward Tobias, and he was hit by a stab of guilt, but that quickly dissipated when something crashed behind him. He whipped his head around to see a giant beam fall to the floor. The house was collapsing.

"I'm sorry," Tobias said. He took the human's left hand and jerked the thumb to the side. The human screamed, but the dislocation allowed Tobias to slip his hand through the shackle. He gritted his teeth as he dislocated the other thumb. The human was free.

Tobias hauled him to his feet. The human stood on his own for only an instant before collapsing, his eyes rolling back into his head. Tobias bit back another curse as he scooped the human up. Thankfully, he wasn't heavy.

Tobias carried him out of the room. His lungs burned, and his limbs trembled as he struggled to put one foot in front of the other. Then his lungs seized with another coughing fit. He couldn't seem to draw in a breath. The air scorched his throat. Tears ran down Tobias's cheeks as he forced himself to take another step. His arms and legs shook. All around him, pieces of the building were falling. The only thing he could hear was the roar of the fire. His entire world became this fiery moment.

Left foot, right foot, left foot, right foot, he repeated like a mantra, forcing himself inch by inch to make his way closer to the stairs. He was almost there when a piece of the ceiling fell down in front of him. He cried out as the sparks flew toward his face, and one of them landed in his eye. It was agony. Tobias reached up to rub his eye, but it only made it worse.

I'm going to die here. He could smell his flesh burning, and the white-hot agony turned to numbness. But then he looked down at the human in his arms and summoned up the last dregs of his strength. He started down the stairs, almost blind from the burning in his eye and the smoke all around him.

Then he fell.

He tumbled down the stairs, his body slamming into hard wood. He lost his grip on the human, who fell farther down than he had. Tobias sobbed while flames licked at his arms and across his back. He had never given much thought to how he would die. He'd vaguely assumed that it would be peaceful, in his sleep, at the ripe old age of 180 or so. He certainly had never considered burning to death while trying to save a human.

Tobias screamed in pain as he struggled down to where the human was. He tried to pat out the flames covering the human's torso, then slung his arm over his shoulders and kept going. This was the last flight of stairs, right? He didn't even know anymore.

He awkwardly made his way down the stairs, his legs shaking as he went. When he reached the bottom, he was greeted by a wall of flames. With his blurry vision, he could just make out what appeared to be the exit. Tobias gave a hysterical laugh as he hobbled toward it. Then the flames hit him. They scorched his entire body, up his neck and across his stomach. He couldn't feel his limbs. He didn't dare look at the human, who must have been in similar shape. With a final burst of strength, he struggled through the door.

The cool air hit him like a ton of bricks, and he collapsed to his knees with a sob. He was alive.

Tobias sent up a prayer of thanks to the goddess before blacking out.

3

Tobias drifted in and out of consciousness.

A flicker of concerned murmuring and a flash of unfamiliar faces gathered around him. Then a stab of pain. He screamed and slipped back into the dark.

All he knew was the pain, the burning that seemed to cover every part of his body—at least the parts he could feel. The rest of him was numb. He couldn't feel his legs or arms.

Tobias blinked his eyes open. A dark wooden ceiling swam into view, but it was blurry. He couldn't see much out of his left eye.

What had happened? He'd been walking home . . .

All at once, it hit him. The fire. The little girl. The human.

His heart rate quickened, and he struggled to sit up.

"He's awake!"

Tobias flinched back from the loud voice. He opened his mouth to ask where he was but was immediately hit by a coughing fit. The coughs seemed to rip his throat apart and hurt his whole body. Tobias was in such agony that he was hardly aware of anything else.

Tears streamed down his face.

"Drink," someone said.

Tobias didn't protest as they raised a cup to his mouth once the coughing had subsided. The blood was lukewarm, but it soothed his throat.

"Please don't try to speak. You inhaled a lot of smoke, and your lungs and throat were damaged."

Tobias looked at the person helping him. All he could make out was a smudge of brown hair and pale skin.

"You're in the burn ward at the hospital. You've been unconscious for the past twelve hours." The doctor encouraged Tobias to lie back down with gentle movements. "You suffered burns across most of your body. You need to rest now, but know that we'll do everything we can to help you."

Tobias tried to nod, but he was already falling asleep.

***

Pain. Tobias jerked away from the person touching his arm and cried out.

"Shh, you're okay. I need to change your bandages."

Tobias looked over at his arm and then wished he hadn't. Even with his blurry vision, he could see that his entire right arm was a mess of raw blistered skin. He watched the blood ooze through the cracks with morbid fascination.

"I'm putting a dressing on that should soothe some of the pain. It needs to be changed every twelve hours for the next couple nights."

Tobias nodded and swallowed. The motion burned his ragged throat.

"H—" he began, then winced. He tried again. "How bad?"

The doctor hesitated. "I'm not going to lie to you. You're lucky to even be alive."

Tobias did not feel lucky at the moment.

"The burns are the worst on your arms and legs, but almost all of your body was affected. Right now, our greatest concern is infection." The doctor paused, as if considering his words. "And your eyes were burned badly as well. The right one is in better shape, but you may never be able to see out of your left eye again."

"Fuck," Tobias whispered.

"Luckily, the burns on your torso are not as severe. I think with proper care, you will recover. Though you will probably be left with some scars."

Tobias's heart skipped a beat. Vampires hardly ever got scars on account of their excellent healing ability. His throat went dry. What would Layla think of him now?

He shook off the thought. "What about the little girl? And the human?"

"The girl sustained only minor injuries. She should make a full recovery."

Tobias sighed with relief.

"The human suffered moderate burns, but he will survive. They surely would have died if you hadn't been there."

***

Tobias did his best to steady his breathing while the doctor changed the bandages around his arms. It fuckin' hurt, and despite his best efforts to stop them, tears streamed down his cheeks. This was his second night at the hospital, and though he was healing, the process was slow and painful.

"Almost done," the doctor said.

Tobias made a little sound of acknowledgement as he looked at the blurry wall. His left eye was covered with bandages. Even with the damaged sight in his right, he had learned that he shouldn't look at what the doctor was doing unless he wanted to lose the contents of his stomach.

"There we go," the doctor said. Tobias turned back to him. "It's healing well so far. No signs of infection."

Tobias nodded as more tears gathered. He was so tired of crying. He closed his eyes and struggled to swallow around the lump in his throat.

"I know this is hard, but you're making good progress. Just try to be patient, all right?"

Tobias didn't respond.

"There is actually someone here to see you."

A jolt went through him. "Who is it?" he asked, hoping it was his friend Layla.

"It's the man whose child and human you saved. Would you like to see him?"

Tobias deflated a bit. Of course Layla wouldn't want to see him when he looked like this. His stomach twisted at the thought of talking to this man. He didn't like attention.

Tobias hesitated but eventually nodded, his curiosity getting the better of him. "Yes, I would."

"I'll send him in. It'll be a quick visit. You need to rest."

The doctor left the room, and a moment later, a finely dressed vampire entered.

"Mr. Tobias Latour, it is an honor," the clean-shaven man said with a bow. "I am Reginald Phinney. My family and I owe you an enormous debt for your bravery."

Tobias shifted uncomfortably. "I just did what I could."

"At great risk to yourself," Phinney added. "You are too modest, Mr. Latour. You are a hero. And a hero deserves a reward."

Phinney pulled up a chair next to Tobias's bed and plopped into it, crossing his ankle over his knee. "I will personally pay for all your medical treatment and help to support you until you can return to work."

Tobias let out a gasp. "Sir, I can't let you do that."

Phinney waved away his objection. "It has already been decided. I've made arrangements with the hospital and have talked to the landlord of your apartment and shop. You don't have to worry about any of that. Just focus on healing."

Tobias wanted to protest. He had never taken a handout in his life, and though he was not rich by any means, he got by. But deep down, he knew that without the income from his work, he would not last long.

"Thank you, Mr. Phinney," Tobias said.

"There is also the issue of your nutritional needs. The doctor tells me that you will have to feed at least twice a night for the foreseeable future. I will provide a human for that purpose, as well as food for that human."

Tobias's heart skipped a beat. A human was a luxury he had never been able to afford, especially with the current human shortage. A human *and* food for them? Well, Tobias didn't know how to respond.

"Th-that's too generous," he said. "Thank you, but I can't accept."

"Nonsense," Phinney said. "You need a human, and I have one to spare. That blood bag you saved from the house is one I've had for years. We were growing tired of his taste and were going to sell him soon to get a new flavor. Really, you'll be doing us a favor by taking him off our hands. And once you're healed, you can keep him if you want, or you can sell him."

"Wasn't he injured too though?" Tobias asked.

"Yes, but his injuries are nowhere near as severe as yours. He should be healed enough to return to his duties by the time you are discharged."

A knock sounded at the door. "It is time for Mr. Latour's medicine," the doctor said.

"Of course." Phinney got to his feet. "It has been a pleasure. Truly. Thank you again, Mr. Latour, from the bottom of my heart."

With that, Phinney swept out of the room. Tobias stared after him, not quite comprehending what had just happened.

The doctor raised a small cup to his lips, and Tobias swallowed the foul liquid. It took all his strength not to retch. Then he drank the cup of blood offered to him and drained every last drop.

4

Bloodbag shivered on the thin mattress. His skin itched, but he wasn't allowed to scratch. He stared up at the ceiling. He was being given away. His new master was the very vampire who had pulled him from the burning house and had suffered severe injuries in the process. Bloodbag had to repay this new master for saving him and thus would be his personal meal as he recovered.

Bloodbag's stomach twisted at the prospect. This new master would surely hate him for making him suffer so. He was sure to beat him, at the very least. He might even whip him.

Bloodbag shuddered at the phantom feeling of a whip striking his back and splitting the skin. His old master had often used the whip when he was displeased with Bloodbag. It had happened a lot in the beginning, but Bloodbag had learned how to be good.

Bloodbag jolted upright at the creaking of the door.

"Come with me."

Bloodbag got to his feet and followed the vampire into the corridor.

"I am taking you to meet your new master," he said without looking at Bloodbag.

Bloodbag followed him through the halls, his stomach aching and his hands trembling with anxiety. The vampire led him into a dim room. There were several beds, but only one was occupied. Bloodbag followed the vampire over to it, his heart pounding so hard he was convinced it would burst.

Master was sleeping. His arms were covered in bandages, as was the left side of his face. He blinked his good eye open. Bloodbag dropped to his knees and bowed his head to the floor, palms on either side. His new master was to be shown all respect, including the posture of submission.

"You must be Bloodbag," Master rasped.

Bloodbag didn't respond—he hadn't been granted permission to speak.

"You can stand up."

Bloodbag obeyed, keeping his eyes lowered at all times. He was being good.

"How are you recovering from your injuries?" Master asked.

Bloodbag took a deep breath. Master clearly expected a verbal response.

"Bloodbag is recovering, Master. The doctors say the burns are well on their way to being healed."

Bloodbag held his breath. Had he said too much? Not enough?

"Good," Master said. Bloodbag waited for him to expand on that, but he didn't. "You'll be going home with me soon."

Bloodbag gave a little nod.

"The doctor said I should start feeding from you now so that the transition is gentler on us both."

Bile rose in Bloodbag's throat, but he pushed it down. He should have expected this.

"Come here." Master held out a hand, and Bloodbag stepped forward. "Give me your arm."

Bloodbag held out his left arm. Goose bumps spread across his skin as Master's cold hand gripped his wrist.

"The doctor said I shouldn't use venom, but I promise I'll be gentle."

Bloodbag nodded. Tears burned at his eyes while he focused on his wrist. Master bent his head down, and Bloodbag caught the glint of white fangs right before pain bit into his wrist. He suppressed a whimper as Master began to feed.

Bloodbag had been at this for a long time, but even still, every time he was fed on, he felt terror. He tried to distract himself by going over everything he knew about Master.

His name was Tobias Latour, and he was a shoemaker. He was young for a vampire, only forty-three. He had selflessly run into the burning house to rescue Master and Mistress's daughter. And then, for reasons Bloodbag could not fathom, he had run back into the house to save him.

Bloodbag's memories of the rescue were hazy. He remembered his terror as the smoke drifted under the door of his cell. He remembered desperately pulling against the shackles and blood streaming down his wrists. He remembered screaming for help until his voice was hoarse. He'd passed out at some point, and then the next thing he knew was an agonizing pain in his hands as his rescuer dislocated his thumbs. After that, all he remembered was smoke clogging his lungs and flames burning his flesh. Then he woke up here, at the hospital.

Fangs pulled out of his flesh, and Master licked his wrist to close the wounds.

"Thank you," Master said simply.

With that, Bloodbag was dismissed and led back to his room. He lay in bed, but he didn't sleep for a long, long time.

***

Tobias watched as Bloodbag was led away. The human had clearly been terrified of him. The way he'd dropped to his knees, how he had hesitated to answer Tobias's questions . . . It was obvious he had not been treated with much kindness by Phinney. As if Tobias needed more proof of that beyond the fact that Bloodbag had been left locked up in a closet.

Tobias sighed, looking up at the ceiling. He'd never understood people who mistreated their humans. Tobias brought his fingers to the pendant around his neck and traced the familiar golden sun—the emblem of Clea.

He hadn't always been one of her followers. Growing up, his family had attended the Temple of Lebne, the god of vampires. But when he was a teenager, Tobias had felt drawn to Clea, the goddess who had saved vampires from starvation by giving them humans to feed on. Some vampires scoffed at the worship of her, saying she wasn't worthy or that her association with the sun made her inaccessible to vampires.

Tobias had never felt that way. Instead, he felt an affinity for the goddess. While Lebne had created his race, Clea had saved it. She was intelligent and kind, and her temple was the most peaceful place Tobias had ever been. When he worshipped the goddess, he felt at home—something he had never felt in all those years worshipping Lebne.

As a follower of Clea, he respected her creatures, the humans whose blood gave him life. They were similar to vampires and yet so different. They didn't live as long, and they weren't as strong, but they could go out in the sun without pain and could survive on many different food sources.

He had always been fascinated by them, but he had never been able to afford one of his own. Now it seemed that Bloodbag would be his human. Tobias had almost died to save him, after all.

Tobias's burned limbs were still bandaged, but the new skin had almost all grown in. That was another thing about humans: they were fragile. They didn't heal fast, and they scarred easily. Tobias would have scars now, despite his enhanced vampire healing. He gently traced one of the raised pink lines that marred his brown arm. He would be stared at. People would whisper about him, ask him what had happened.

He closed his eyes as his mind filled with the image of the burning structure, the flames swirling around him. He could almost feel his skin burning all over again, the scent of roasting flesh clogging his nose.

Tobias balled the sheets in his hands. He forced himself to take a breath. It was shaky. He took another. Slowly, the pounding of his heart quieted. Tobias relaxed his hands.

He was safe. He was here in the hospital, healing. He would be able to go home soon. The flames couldn't get him now. They were gone. He was safe.

5

—◦—

"Well, Mr. Latour, I think you're ready for discharge," the doctor said.

Tobias's heart leapt into his throat. He had been in the hospital for three nights, and now he was being sent back into the world.

"Thank you," Tobias said. "For everything."

"You're welcome." The doctor clasped one of Tobias's hands in both of his. "If you ever need anything, you know where to find me."

It was odd changing out of his hospital clothes. Tobias pulled on a pair of trousers and a shirt, wincing at the tightness in his shoulder. The fabric was rough against his skin in comparison to the hospital gown. His muscles protested as he bent to put on his stockings and boots.

When he was dressed, he walked out of the room and to the front entryway of the facility. The hallways were empty, which he silently thanked the goddess for.

Bloodbag waited for him in the foyer. He was dressed simply, his jacket and boots clearly too big. He wore a dark leather collar around his neck, as was required of all humans. As soon as he saw Tobias, he dropped down in submission. Unease prickled in Tobias's stomach.

"Are you ready, Bloodbag?" he asked. He didn't like that name, but apparently, it was what the human was used to.

"Yes, Master," Bloodbag said softly.

"Well, let's go."

Bloodbag got to his feet. He kept his eyes lowered as they exited the building and climbed into a waiting carriage. Tobias climbed in first and settled onto one of the seats. Bloodbag followed but didn't sit down. His eyes flicked between the seats. Then Bloodbag sank to his knees on the floor of the carriage.

Tobias had not expected that.

The carriage started rolling. They hit a bump, and Tobias winced at the thought of how it had felt on Bloodbag's knees. "You can sit on the seat," he said.

Bloodbag looked up at him in confusion. Just then, they hit another big bump. Bloodbag pitched forward, his forehead cracking on Tobias's knee. Tobias let out a hiss of pain.

"Bloodbag is sorry, Master!" Bloodbag cried, cowering back. He was shaking. "Bloodbag is so very, very sorry."

"It's all right," Tobias said. "Please, sit in the seat."

Bloodbag scrambled up into the seat across from Tobias. He clasped his hands in his lap and kept his eyes lowered.

The rest of the ride passed in awkward silence. The scent of fear radiated off Bloodbag and put Tobias on edge. He released a breath of relief when the carriage finally rolled to a stop in front of his home.

***

Bloodbag knew he was going to be punished. He had hurt Master. That would have earned him at least ten lashes with the whip from his previous master and the muzzle for a week. A completely reasonable punishment, one that taught Bloodbag how to behave. Bloodbag was stupid—he knew that—and that was why the vampires used pain to make sure he understood when he did something wrong. Even though Bloodbag had earned this punishment and knew it was necessary, the thought of it still filled his veins with dread.

He wondered how this new master preferred to punish his humans. He had a stern face, one that always seemed to be on the edge of a frown. He'd been gentle with Bloodbag so far, but Bloodbag was under no illusions that that would continue.

"Bloodbag, come," Master said.

Bloodbag jumped. He hadn't realized they had reached their destination. Master was already standing outside the carriage with a deep frown on his face. Bloodbag scrambled out of the carriage, nearly tripping over his own feet.

Without a word, Master led him up a flight of steps. He unlocked the door, and Bloodbag followed him inside.

"Take your shoes off," Master said.

Bloodbag quickly did as he was told. He gathered his boots in his hands and stood still, staring at his stockinged feet as Master removed his own shoes.

"Thank you," Master said, taking the shoes from Bloodbag's hands.

Bloodbag dropped his hands so they were clasped in front of him.

"You're free to roam around the house as you like," Master said. "I'll find you before dawn for feeding."

And with that, Master left him. Bloodbag stood there, every muscle tense. What about his punishment?

He waited for several minutes, unsure what to do. Maybe this was the punishment? Master making him wait, giving him time to grow even more anxious about how he would pay. Yes, that had to be it.

Bloodbag hesitantly raised his head to take in his surroundings.

He stood in a narrow hallway with worn rugs lining the floor. Master had gone up the staircase directly in front of him. Bloodbag bit his lip before slowly making his way down the hall. He peeked in the door on the right. It was so dark he could hardly make anything out, but he thought there might be an armchair and fireplace. Farther down the hall, he found a tiny room with a stove and a couple cabinets.

Besides that, the only other things on the first floor were a closet and the front door. Bloodbag opened the closet. It had a bucket, a mop, a broom, and some rags.

Master will want Bloodbag to clean, he thought. His previous master was wealthy and had employed multiple vampire servants to take care of his house. But it was clear that this master was not rich.

Bloodbag was hit by a stab of guilt. No, he shouldn't think that of his master.

He quickly shut the closet door, then walked down the hall and entered the living room. He would wait there for Master to come feed.

6

Tobias ran his hand over his bed. The soft sheets smelled so familiar. He had missed being home. At the same time, he almost felt like a stranger in the space. He couldn't move freely like he once had; his bones and muscles and joints and skin ached.

He'd changed in that fire, and he didn't like it. Tobias sighed as he lay back in bed. He didn't have the energy he used to have. It wasn't even midnight, and already, he needed a nap. Just a couple minutes . . . Tobias's eyes drifted closed.

Crash.

Tobias jolted upright at the sound, his heart pounding. It took him a moment to realize he was at home. The sound had come from downstairs.

Shit. Bloodbag. Tobias scrambled out of bed and hurried to the stairs, wincing at the tightness in his legs.

"Bloodbag?" he called. No response. He frowned and walked down the steps and into the small sitting room. It was dim, but he immediately spotted the shattered vase on the floor, where water had soaked into the rug.

Tobias's eyes snapped up when he heard a whimper. Bloodbag knelt in the corner of the room, shaking.

"What happened?" Tobias asked.

"B-Bloodbag didn't mean to, Master! It was dark. Bloodbag couldn't see. Bloodbag is stupid and clumsy, Master. Bloodbag is sorry."

Of course. Tobias had forgotten that humans couldn't see well in the dark. He should have provided Bloodbag with a candle.

"It's all right," he said. "Can you come over here?" Tobias would have gone to him, but his legs were beginning to tremble. He sank down into the plush chair.

Bloodbag crawled over to him. A wave of disgust hit Tobias—not directed at Bloodbag, but at the people who had conditioned him to believe he was nothing more than an animal. Bloodbag pressed his forehead to the floor in front of Tobias.

"Bloodbag has been bad," he said, his voice barely above a whisper. "Bloodbag will accept his punishment."

Tobias stared down at him. It was common practice for vampires to forcefully discipline their humans, but he couldn't bring himself to even consider hurting the poor creature.

"I'm not going to punish you," Tobias said as gently as he could.

Bloodbag stilled. A new scent drifted off of him, stronger than fear. It was terror.

"Bloodbag, why are you scared? I just said I'm not going to hurt you."

Bloodbag hesitated a moment before he responded. "Thank you, Master."

"You're welcome. I do want you to clean up the mess. There should be a bucket and rags in the back closet that you can use."

"Of course, Master. Bloodbag will do that right away." Bloodbag crawled out of the room, only getting to his feet once he was on the other side of the door. Tobias heard him run down the hall. He felt a stab of guilt at making Bloodbag clean it up, but he was too weak to do it himself.

Bloodbag came back into the room with the supplies.

"You can light a candle," Tobias said. "There should be one in the drawer in the corner."

"Yes, Master. Thank you, Master."

Bloodbag quickly found and lit the candle. He carefully set it on the table, then got to his knees to clean up the mess. He picked up the shards of broken ceramic and dropped them into the bucket, along with the flowers. He was meticulous.

Then he used the rags to mop up the water. Once he was done, he set the wet rags in the bucket, then returned to his submissive posture.

"Bloodbag has cleaned up the mess, Master."

"I can see that," Tobias said. "Good work, Bloodbag."

The tension in Bloodbag's body and the scent of his fear on the air made it clear Bloodbag still expected to be punished.

"I need to feed," Tobias said. "Please come here."

Bloodbag complied. He knelt at Tobias's feet and kept his eyes on the floor. Tobias scooted over in his chair. "Climb up."

Bloodbag hesitantly climbed into the chair next to Tobias. There was no way they could avoid touching, and Tobias maneuvered him so that Bloodbag's legs hung over the arm of the chair. Bloodbag let Tobias move him around so he could get a better angle. While he did, Bloodbag's eyes grew distant, and his body went as limp as a rag doll. It was creepy.

Tobias rubbed Bloodbag's back. "You are very good at cleaning," he said softly. "I'm lucky to have such a diligent human."

Bloodbag didn't respond to the praise. Tobias frowned and examined Bloodbag more closely. The human stared at some point over Tobias's shoulder. His breathing was shaky. His heart was beating too fast. Something was clearly wrong with him.

"Bloodbag?" Tobias said. No response. It was like he couldn't hear him, like he was trapped under the ice, completely frozen.

Tobias had heard of this before: humans who became unresponsive when they were fed on. It was supposedly something to do with being prey animals. He sighed as he brushed a bit of hair out of Bloodbag's face.

"I won't hurt you," he whispered.

He bit down on Bloodbag's neck. Bloodbag jerked in Tobias's arms and let out a little cry, but then the venom hit, and his body went limp. Tobias cradled him close as he fed. The blood was hot and rich and slid down his throat easily. Tobias almost sobbed. He hadn't realized how hungry he was. The doctor had told him he would have to feed much more often, but he hadn't had the chance to become hungry at the hospital. Now, though, he was ravenous.

Tobias drank deeply, all the while gently rubbing Bloodbag's arm. It was as much to give himself comfort as Bloodbag. The human had slipped into unconsciousness under the influence of the venom.

Tobias gasped when he'd filled his stomach. He licked the punctures on Bloodbag's neck closed. With a full belly and a warm body next to his, Tobias settled back in his chair and closed his eyes. He needed a nap.

7

Bloodbag gradually came awake with a crick in his neck and his back and, well, everywhere. He went to stretch only to realize he wasn't alone. Bloodbag snapped his eyes open to see that he was in Master's lap, with the vampire's arm clutched tightly around him.

Bloodbag looked at the arm for a long minute. He was trapped. He couldn't move or he would wake Master. Bloodbag glanced up at Master's face. His skin was a light brown, and faint crow's feet were beginning to form around his eyes. He had a short cropped black beard. Master looked kinder in his sleep. When he was awake, he was stern and serious, but sleep softened that.

Master had saved his life, but Bloodbag had no idea why he had risked his own life for a worthless human. Bloodbag would try to be on his best behavior for Master.

He hadn't been punished yet—not for his blunder in the carriage and not for the broken vase. Bloodbag knew the punishment was coming though. The punishment always came.

Master shifted, and a spike of fear went through him.

"You're awake."

Bloodbag jumped at Master's voice.

Master chuckled. "I didn't mean to frighten you," he said. "You can climb down."

Bloodbag slipped off Master's lap to kneel at his feet, every muscle straining in anticipation of the coming pain. Master was silent for a long moment.

"Bloodbag, can you tell me why you're scared?"

Bloodbag thought hard about what Master was asking. It seemed Master wanted him to recount all his mistakes aloud before beginning his punishment.

"Because Bloodbag was bad. Bloodbag hurt Master and broke Master's property. Bloodbag is waiting for Master's punishment."

"Did . . . your old master punish you?" Master asked.

Bloodbag blinked at the question. Of course he had punished him.

"Yes," Bloodbag said. "Master punished Bloodbag so Bloodbag would learn to be good." He sensed tension radiating off Master and cringed back from him.

"How did he punish you?" Master asked.

Bloodbag's throat had gone dry. His voice came out scratchy. "Many ways, Master. He would hit Bloodbag often, though sometimes he would whip Bloodbag if Bloodbag had been really bad. When Bloodbag was too bad, Master shackled Bloodbag. He would muzzle Bloodbag during the day so that he and Mistress would be able to sleep and not hear Bloodbag's pathetic noises."

Master cursed, and Bloodbag's stomach dropped. Master must've been angry he had been given such a troublesome human.

"But Bloodbag has learned, Master," he rushed to say, desperation clawing at his throat. "Bloodbag will be good for you! Bloodbag will accept any punishment you decide to use, Master. Bloodbag will learn to be better. Bloodbag promises."

Bloodbag's head pressed against the floor, and he was sobbing now, his dirty tears falling onto Master's carpet, another thing he would no doubt be punished for.

A hand settled atop his head. Bloodbag braced himself, but Master didn't pull his hair or pinch him or slap him. Instead, he gently ran his fingers through Bloodbag's hair.

"I'm sorry you were hurt so much," he said. "I'm not going to punish you."

Bloodbag's forehead wrinkled in confusion. "Bloodbag doesn't understand, Master."

"I'm not going to punish you for the things you've done. I'm never going to punish you. Ever."

Bloodbag's heart skipped a beat. That could only mean one thing.

Master was going to kill him or sell him, which would ultimately lead to his death.

"Please, Master," Bloodbag said, his voice breaking. "Bloodbag will be good. Bloodbag can be punished. Bloodbag knows Bloodbag is worthless, an animal, but Bloodbag can be taught. Bloodbag will take whatever punishment you decide on. Bloodbag can be useful. Please, Master, please don't kill this worthless human."

Bloodbag didn't even know if Master could hear him, he was sobbing so hard. His pulse roared in his ears.

"Bloodbag, I believe that you can be good."

Bloodbag quieted his sobs and let out a deep breath as a tiny bit of his anxiety dissipated.

"Look at me."

Bloodbag sat back on his knees so that he could look at Master. He didn't look at his face, of course—he was stupid, but he wasn't *that* stupid. Instead, he looked at Master's chest.

"Your punishment is that you will not eat tonight. It's almost dawn, so you will sleep in this room on the floor today. If you are good, I will give you food when the sun goes down. Do you understand?"

"Yes, Master. Bloodbag understands the punishment. Thank you for teaching Bloodbag how to be better." Bloodbag's muscles relaxed, and his crying softened. He was being punished. Not in the same way his old master had punished him, but he was being punished nonetheless. Master was teaching him to be good.

"Very well." Master stood. "I am going to bed." Without another word, he left the room, blowing out the candle on his way.

Bloodbag slumped to the floor. His stomach ached from hunger, but he had felt worse. He curled up on the floor. The whole room was piled with rugs and carpets. It was more comfortable than Bloodbag's cell back at his old master's, but it wasn't as comfortable as the bed at the hospital. It was a suitable punishment after Bloodbag had been spoiled for the past few days. Master surely wouldn't allow his human to live in luxury at his house.

8

— • —

Tobias felt sick to his stomach as he left Bloodbag on the floor of the sitting room. Bloodbag truly believed he deserved to be punished for accidents, to be beaten or whipped. He had actually knelt in front of Tobias, begging to be punished because he thought the only alternative was being killed.

Forgive me, Goddess, he prayed. He hoped Bloodbag would be okay without food and sleeping on the floor. He'd needed to punish him somehow, just to alleviate his terror, and that had been the gentlest form of "punishment" Tobias could bring himself to dole out.

He closed the door to his room and changed for bed. The blood had made him feel better, but he was already starting to feel hungry again. He would have to be careful and make sure he didn't take too much from Bloodbag. The human was also still recovering from burns and, based on how skinny he was, starvation as well.

Tobias sighed. He didn't know if he had the strength to do this. Bloodbag was his now. Legally, he could do whatever he wanted with him. But in his heart, Tobias knew he was not—and would never be—the kind of master Bloodbag was used to having, and he worried that was the kind of master Bloodbag believed he needed.

"Disgusting," Tobias muttered, filled with rage at the thought of what that bastard Phinney had done to him. He was never going to let Bloodbag near that vampire again.

Tobias sucked in a breath as he pulled his shirt over his head. The skin on his shoulders was still tight and tender. He paused a moment to look in the mirror.

His skin was dull, with pink scars trailing along his upper arms, shoulders, and back. There were more on his legs. His traced his fingers along the scars on his left arm. He had almost died. He closed his eyes as fear bubbled to the surface.

I'm safe. I'm safe. He tried to calm his racing heart and ease the twisting in his stomach with the mantra. The doctor had said the anxiety was normal, that it would fade with time. But it fuckin' sucked.

Tobias sank down onto his bed and covered his face with his hands. Silent sobs shook his shoulders. So much had changed so quickly. His body was weak and in shambles. He now owned a human, one who had clearly been through hell. It was all too much.

Tobias curled up on his side and pulled a pillow against his stomach. He didn't know what would happen next, when he would be well enough to return to work, or when his body would stop aching every second of every day. He was exhausted.

He must have dozed off at some point, because the next time Tobias opened his eyes, afternoon light was peeking in around the curtains. His stomach rumbled.

Tobias sat up, his joints aching. He reached up to rub at his eye and stopped himself just in time. He gritted his teeth. The doctor had told him that if he was to have any hope of his left eye recovering, he couldn't touch it.

Tobias padded across the room and grabbed a robe. He didn't have the energy to put on real clothes. Tonight he would see about getting Bloodbag settled in.

The stairs creaked as Tobias made his way down. He took a steadying breath before he entered the sitting room to find Bloodbag curled up right where he'd left him, one arm underneath his head like a pillow. His neck was bare. Tobias approached him.

The human's neck was covered in scars—so many he couldn't even attempt to count them. He seemed a bit old for a human, maybe in his late thirties. Tobias spotted a couple gray hairs, but the human's hair was mostly dark brown. It was striking against his pale skin.

Tobias couldn't bring himself to wake Bloodbag, so he set off to the back of the house to get him some food. He had never had to feed a human before, but Phinney had sent over premade foods to make it easy. The man was a piece of shit in many ways, but at least he was helping Tobias feed his new human.

Most vampire houses didn't have a full kitchen, and Tobias's was no exception. The room was tiny, only big enough for a small stove and a cabinet for storing a kettle, a couple glasses, and some jarred blood.

On that shelf sat about half a dozen packages wrapped in brown paper. Tobias examined the closest one. *Cheese*, it said. The next one was *Bread*, and the one next to it was *Apples*. There was also *Salted Beef*, *Carrots*, and *Grapes*.

He stared at the food in bewilderment. It seemed like a lot, but he had no idea how much humans ate in a day. He hesitantly opened the apple package and took out one of the red spheres. It felt odd in his hand, the smoothness unlike anything he was used to. He then grabbed a strip of beef. This felt more familiar, similar to the leather he worked with at his shop.

Satisfied with his choices, Tobias made his way back to the sitting room. Bloodbag stirred as he approached. His eyes blinked open groggily. He gave a little squeak when he saw Tobias and scrambled up into a kneeling position.

"It's okay," Tobias said. "I didn't mean to startle you. I brought you food." He awkwardly held out the apple and beef. Bloodbag didn't move to take it, but he licked his lips. "Your punishment is over. You can eat now."

Bloodbag took the food from Tobias. "Thank you, Master."

"You're welcome. Once you are done eating, come find me."

Tobias left the room. A short time later, Bloodbag appeared in the doorway to his small library.

"Did you get enough to eat?" Tobias asked.

"Yes, Master. Thank you, Master," Bloodbag said.

"Good. Come with me. I'll show you your room."

Tobias led Bloodbag down the hallway. "It's not big, but it should be comfortable for you." He opened the door to the small extra bedroom that was usually reserved for guests. There was a bed in one corner, a chair, and a set of drawers. Bloodbag froze.

Tobias turned back to him with a frown. "Don't you like it?"

"Yes, Master, yes. Thank you for your generosity." Bloodbag took a couple steps into the room. He looked around like he was searching for something. "Master . . . where are the chains?"

Tobias bit back a bitter reply. He considered his words carefully. "You're healing from burns too, and I think it is best not to chain you until you are completely healed. And even then, to me it seems like the chains are unnecessary."

Bloodbag nodded. "Thank you, Master," he whispered.

"I need to feed now."

Bloodbag nodded, turning to face Tobias, his eyes downcast. Tobias took his hand and led him to the bed. Bloodbag sat down, and Tobias sat down next to him. He brushed a bit of hair away from Bloodbag's neck, then bit down hard and fast. As Bloodbag slumped from the venom, Tobias drank greedily. There were tears in his eyes as the pangs in his stomach finally started to ease.

Tobias drank until he couldn't take anymore. He licked the wounds closed and laid Bloodbag down on the bed. Bloodbag's eyes were unfocused, and he stared past Tobias. He looked a little pale.

"Thank you," Tobias said. "I'll go get you some water."

Bloodbag was in no position to argue, sedated as he was by the venom. Tobias returned shortly with a glass of water, but Bloodbag was dozing. He gave him a gentle shake. Bloodbag opened his eyes and gave Tobias a little smile. Tobias smiled back.

"Water," Tobias said gently. He helped Bloodbag sit up and drink. The human's limbs were limp, but he managed a couple swallows. Tobias laid him back down and covered him with a blanket. Bloodbag's eyes closed again, and his breathing evened out.

Watching him, Tobias was hit by a burst of protectiveness. He would never let this human be hurt by anyone ever again.

9

—— • ——

Tobias winced as he unwrapped the bandages from around his arm. His skin was painful to the touch and itchy at the same time. The burn on his arm seemed to spill across his skin.

He had almost died.

It still didn't feel real to him, the way his life had changed so quickly. He had always taken his body for granted, and now it was broken in so many ways.

He had almost died, and what did he have to show for his life? Nothing but a moderately successful cobbler shop. Tobias gritted his teeth as he wrapped the fresh bandage around his arm. The idea of returning to his shop left a sour taste in his mouth. He couldn't see himself continuing to mend shoes for the rest of his life, never doing anything worthwhile.

His parents had moved back to Enrone when he was twenty. He'd been born and raised in Cesvic and hadn't wanted to move to a foreign country, so his father left him the cobbler shop, and Tobias had kept it running for the last twenty-three years for no reason except for the work was easy and paid the bills.

For years, there had been a feeling nagging at him. That his life was meant for so much more. That just because he was good at mending shoes didn't mean that was the only thing he could ever do.

Tobias reached up and fiddled with his pendant. *Tell me what to do, Clea.* His mind drifted back to the temple—the candles, the perfume of incense, the peace.

He wanted peace.

The monks at the temple always seemed content, even happy. They worshipped the goddess, and they cared for those in need, both vampire and human. They made a difference.

His fingers stilled. What if that was what he was called to do? Join the Order, live as a monk in service to the goddess?

If someone had told him he should join the Order a week ago, he would have laughed and shook his head. *No*, he would have said. *I have a shop to run, responsibilities.* But now, after the fire that had almost killed him, the shop seemed inconsequential.

He didn't want to die and leave behind a meaningless legacy.

A knock sounded at the door. Tobias's heart leapt into his throat.

Layla.

He made his way downstairs and opened the door.

"Tobias!" Layla squeezed him into a hug.

Tobias gasped at the flare of pain against his skin, but he wrapped his arms around her anyway, relaxing just a fraction at her familiar scent.

"I missed you," Layla murmured.

"I missed you too," he said. He pressed a gentle kiss against her lips. "Come inside." He helped her remove her coat, his breath catching when he saw the low-cut burgundy dress she was wearing. She was stunning as ever, with pale skin and waves of black hair. He wrapped his arms around her waist and pressed a kiss against her bare shoulder.

She laughed. "Really, Tobias, I think we should catch up before we start all that."

"Fine," Tobias said, giving her a smile. "But I can't wait to ravish you."

He led her to the sitting room, where she settled onto the sofa, and he poured them both glasses of wine. He sat down next to her.

"How have you been doing?" she asked.

Tobias shrugged. "I've been better. But most of the burns are healing, and I'm slowly getting my energy back."

"I was so worried," she said softly. She rested her hand on his forearm. "I don't know what I would do if I lost you."

"You'll never lose me, darling."

Their relationship was an odd one. Tobias had only met Layla because she came into his shop to pick up some shoes her mother had ordered. She came from a wealthy family, way above Tobias's station in life. But the attraction had been instant for both of them. Now they'd been dating for close to twenty years.

"How have you been?" he asked.

"Better now that I'm with you," she said. "Let's go upstairs."

Tobias let her pull him to his feet and lead him to the bedroom. As soon as the door was closed, she was kissing him, her hands roaming over his body. Tobias growled deep in his throat as he kissed her back, teasing the tips of her fangs with his tongue.

They undressed each other and fell into bed. Then everything was fangs and skin and sweat and currents of pleasure.

Tobias collapsed afterward, sweat dripping down his face. "Damn, Layla." He exhaled. "I forgot how fuckin' amazing you are in bed."

Layla laughed and gave him a kiss on the cheek. "Well, I don't think you'll forget again anytime soon."

He rolled over onto his side so he could look at her. She was beautiful.

"I'm sorry," he whispered.

A crease appeared between her brows. "What for?"

Tobias closed his eyes. "For the scars. I know they're ugly."

Layla didn't respond. Tears pricked the backs of Tobias's eyes.

Then a kiss landed on his shoulder. Tobias opened his eyes in surprise.

Layla planted another kiss on one of his largest scars. "I love them," she said. "Because if you didn't have them, you'd be dead. And you're still gorgeous."

A warm blush rose to his cheeks.

"I have to go," Layla said. "I'll see you tomorrow night?"

"Absolutely." Tobias gave her a quick peck on the lips before she left the room.

10

— · —

Tobias stood in front of the Temple of Clea, hesitating outside the doors. It felt as though once he opened them, he would be stepping into a new life with no way back.

I'm just going to talk to a monk. Just talk. But what if it was more than that?

Tobias groaned in frustration before opening the doors and stepping inside. One step at a time.

The temple was quiet at this time of night. Tobias walked across the marble floor, inhaling deeply as the scent of incense washed over him. He stopped just before the altar, staring up at the statue of the goddess. He knelt to pray. *Thank you for sparing my life and the life of Bloodbag. Thank you for saving us from the flames.*

Fire was under Clea's domain, just as water was under Lebne's. Tobias had no doubts that without the goddess's protection, they both would have perished that night.

A stab of guilt went through him. *I'm sorry for not being able to help him.* Tobias was so, so sorry. All he wanted was for Bloodbag not to be scared, but he still was, and it seemed to be getting worse. The human was constantly on edge, and Tobias had no idea what to do.

He opened his eyes at the sound of footsteps. One of the monks had approached the altar and was lighting candles along the back. Tobias watched her silently. She was an older woman, with gray hair pulled back in a loose bun. She looked calm, at peace. Tobias sighed. He wished he could feel peace.

"I'm surprised to see you here," the monk said.

Tobias jumped a little. He hadn't realized she had noticed him.

"I heard about the fire. That was very brave of you."

"Some people say that. Others say it was incredibly stupid."

The monk gave a quiet chuckle. "In any case, most people wouldn't have done what you did. The goddess certainly protected you."

Tobias nodded, a lump rising in his throat. "What's your name?"

"Mora."

"Mora," Tobias said. "Will you pray with me?"

"Of course." Mora knelt beside Tobias.

Tobias started with the litany, and Mora joined him. The words were familiar, calming, and for the first time in many nights, Tobias began to truly relax. He had always found prayer to have that effect.

When they finished, they knelt there in silence for a few minutes. Tobias licked his lips, and fresh anxiety swirled within him.

"Why did you join the Order?" he asked finally.

"I couldn't imagine myself doing anything else," Mora said with a shrug. "I've loved the goddess since I was a little girl, and I knew I wanted to dedicate my life to her."

Tobias pondered that. "I . . . also feel a strong love for the goddess," he said eventually. "I just don't know what she wants me to do." He took a deep breath. "I feel like I might be being called to the Order, but I'm not sure." He had never spoken these thoughts out loud. Hell, he had only admitted to himself what he was feeling last night.

Mora gave him a kind look. "Sometimes the goddess's voice is quiet. It's okay if it takes a while to hear exactly what she is telling you."

Tobias nodded. "The human I saved in the fire . . . his owner gave him to me. And I'd never owned a human before, so I had no idea what to expect. He seems to be terrified of me, and no matter what I do, he's always afraid." Tobias's voice broke. "I feel like I'm failing her. Clea. Like I should be able to help him. But his owner tortured him for years, and sometimes it seems like there isn't even a person left inside him."

Mora closed her eyes, and a flicker of pain flashed across her face. "In my years at the temple, we have taken in dozens of humans. Each one has a unique history. Some are fresh from the villages; others have had kind owners, others cruel. Some of them quickly learn that they are safe here and relax. Others have been abused so much that they can't fathom a life where they aren't hurt. They still shake and cry whenever a vampire gets close, or they won't let us near them at all. They'll curse and fight. The worst, though, are those who have gone numb. They will let you do anything to them. They don't talk, don't react. They just stare at the wall."

"That's awful," Tobias said.

"It is. But no matter what, we treat our humans gently and with respect. Sometimes they heal, and sometimes they don't. A lot of that is outside our control. Our job is to give them a safe life. Eventually, most of them realize they are truly safe here. The ones who don't, well, we make sure they are as comfortable as possible. Sometimes that means giving in to their training, calling them by an identification number or letting them sleep on the floor.

"It's hard for that not to feel like a defeat. But the way I look at it, I would rather have a human sleep on the floor in a warm room than sleep chained in a freezing basement." Mora met his eyes. "You have to pick your battles. And for so many of these humans, anything is better than where they were before."

Tobias nodded. "Thank you," he whispered.

"You're welcome. If you ever need help, we are here to assist." Mora stood. "If you'll excuse me, I have some things to attend to."

"Of course. Thank you for talking to me."

Mora nodded to him and turned to walk away. Then she stopped, looking back at him. "And, Tobias? From what you've told me, I don't think you're failing the goddess. If anything, I think you're making her proud to count you as one of her followers."

Tobias's heart ached. "Thank you," he said with sincerity.

Mora gave him a small smile as she left.

11

—·—

Tobias sighed as he stared at the ceiling. Layla slept next to him, her head nuzzled against his shoulder. He needed to do something, anything, because what he had been trying to do—get back to normal as quickly as possible—wasn't working.

His thoughts drifted back to his conversation with Mora. She had seemed so at peace, so happy. He wanted to feel happy again. He hadn't been for a very, very long time.

"Hi, handsome."

Tobias looked over at Layla, her hair tangled from sleep, her lipstick smeared from their passionate lovemaking. He had never seen something so beautiful.

"Good evening, beautiful." He pressed a kiss to her lips.

Layla sighed into the kiss, her hand stroking his chest. She pulled back and gave him a smile. But then her brow furrowed. "What's wrong?" she asked, cupping his cheek with her hand.

Tobias put his hand over hers. He hadn't realized he was crying. "I'm just so tired. Tired of being in pain and the looks I get when I leave the house and the feeling that nothing will ever change."

"Oh, Tobias." She pressed a gentle kiss to his cheek. "I'm sorry. How can I help?"

Tobias just shook his head. "I don't know. I don't know what to do."

He clutched the pendant around his neck and rubbed his thumb across the familiar shape—the sun with its rays spreading out to touch all those living.

"I've been feeling a calling for a long time, but I didn't know what it meant. I . . . I think the goddess might want me to join the Order."

She answered with a loud snort. "You can't be serious." Layla laughed, and Tobias stared at her. "Wait, really?"

"Yes, really," Tobias said shortly.

Layla sat up in bed, clutching the sheets to her chest. "Tobias, I say this with love, but that is the most ridiculous thing I have ever heard."

Anger and hurt lanced through him. Layla continued.

"I know your faith is important to you, so I've never said anything, but everybody knows only fools worship Clea. And you are not a fool."

It was like she had slapped him. Tobias gripped his pendant tighter as rage built.

"I can't believe you would say that," he said, his voice low.

"Please don't get mad. I just want what's best for you." She placed her hand on his leg. "And I don't think joining a religious order is it. You can do so much more with your life than that."

Her expression was sincere, but tears pricked at Tobias's eyes. He had never thought Layla could be this cruel.

"Can you help me understand? Why are you thinking about this?"

Tobias took a deep breath as he tried to steady his raging emotions. He struggled to think clearly, to put the feelings that had been swirling through his soul into words.

"I've hardly ever felt a moment of peace in my life. When I was seven years old, I joined my parents at the shop, attended school sporadically. When they moved back to Enrone, I took over the management of the shop. And it's been that way for twenty years. Every year, every day, the same thing. The same worries about money. The same job." He closed his eyes as tears rolled down his cheeks. "I need a purpose," he whispered. "I need more than just making shoes."

"Oh, babe," Layla said. "There are other ways of finding your purpose."

Tobias shook his head. "You don't understand. I feel it in my soul, that this is the only way. That this is what I need to do."

Before he'd started this conversation, he wasn't sure. But the feeling was growing, and it was so strong behind his breastbone that it was hard to breathe. He needed to join the monks of Clea.

"You'll be leaving everything behind, Tobias. Your shop, which you have spent your whole life growing. Your house. Your friends. Me." Her voice broke. "You can't leave me. Please, Tobias." She rested her hands against his chest as she kissed him desperately. "Please don't do this. Don't leave me. I know things have been hard for you lately, but this is not the solution. You need to heal. You can't make a life-changing decision like this in the midst of trauma. You'll just regret it."

"I've been thinking about this for years," Tobias said. "Years, Layla. This isn't just something I thought up on a whim. I've talked to the monks at the temple, and I know this is what I need to do."

Layla pulled back from him, her mouth a thin line. "I can't believe you." She climbed out of bed and started pulling on her clothes. "I can't fuckin' believe you. After all we've been through." She stomped to the door and pulled it open.

Tobias jumped out of bed. "Layla, wait."

She spun on him. "I've been with you through everything, Tobias. Everything! Your parents leaving, your moods, this!" She gestured toward him. "And you're just going to leave me like that."

Tobias took a step back.

"Well, I'm done, Tobias. Done. You've never been anything but a selfish prick. And that fire ruined you." She sneered. "Did you actually believe that I don't care about the scars? Scars are for humans, not vampires. You're damaged goods. I stood by you because we've been together so long, but I can't be with a human fucker anymore."

Tobias gasped at the slur. He gaped at her. "Go," he snapped. "Just go."

Without another word, Layla turned on her heel and left.

Tobias sank to the floor. He'd thought Layla cared about him. All of him. But she obviously didn't, not really. He put his head in his hands as he sobbed.

"Master?"

Tobias snapped his head up to where Bloodbag stood in the doorway.

"Are . . . Are you all right?"

Tobias just shook his head. Bloodbag hesitated, but then he made his way into the room. He sank to his knees next to him. The next thing Tobias knew, Bloodbag's arms were wrapped around him in a crushing hug. Tobias hiccupped as he wrapped his own arms around Bloodbag.

"How much did you hear?" he asked.

"Just the shouting," Bloodbag said.

Tobias sighed. "I've been with Layla for decades. But it's like we never even knew each other at all."

12

It had been a week since Tobias brought Bloodbag home. A week. And still Bloodbag was on edge constantly. He was obedient; that wasn't the problem. The problem was that he reeked of anxiety. And him being anxious was making Tobias anxious.

That was why Tobias sent a message to Matthew. He was the only person he knew who had substantial experience with humans, including those who had been mistreated in the past.

"Thanks for coming," Tobias said, closing the door to his small office.

Matthew settled in a chair, legs crossed. "Of course. Anything for a friend. How are you holding up?"

Tobias sighed. It seemed like everyone wanted to know that. "Things have been hard," he admitted. "But I hope that once I get this stuff with Bloodbag sorted out, it'll get better. How are things at the café?"

Matthew ran a hand through his hair. "They've been better. I assume you've heard about the human shortage?"

Tobias nodded. The whole city had been talking about it. An outbreak of disease at Cesvic's primary blood butcher had killed almost a third of the humans in the blood supply. Blood prices had skyrocketed across the city, leaving people scared and hungry.

"The government confiscated half my humans."

Tobias gasped. "That's awful! Do you know if they're all right?"

Matthew shook his head. "The authorities said they'll be returned once the emergency has passed, but I don't have high hopes. Their bodies won't be able to keep up with the amount of blood they have to give." Matthew's voice broke. "I only have ten—no, nine—humans now, and I have to turn customers away because the humans are losing too much blood. I already lost one to blood loss." Matthew's grief was palpable. He loved his humans and tried to provide the best life possible for them.

"I'm so sorry." Tobias couldn't image how awful this whole situation was for him. "Please let me know if there's anything I can do to help."

"Thanks." Matthew wiped his eyes with his sleeve and cleared his throat. "What's going on with Bloodbag?"

It took Tobias a moment to bring himself back to the reason he'd asked Matthew to come visit. His problems seemed insignificant in comparison with Matthew's, and embarrassment heated his face.

"He's constantly on edge. Anxious at the very least, if not outright terrified. He will only refer to himself as 'Bloodbag,' and I hate using that as his name, but I'm afraid that using something else will make him even more nervous. He thinks he deserves to be punished for any perceived slight, and he literally asked me where the chains were. I don't know what to do."

Tobias put his head in his hands. "I feel like an awful person. I want to help him, but I don't know how, and it seems easier to just let things continue the way they have been. We're both still recovering from the fire, and even though he doesn't say anything, I know he's in pain. Meanwhile, I'm so weak that I can hardly walk down the stairs some days."

Tobias wanted to cry, but he had done so much crying over the past week that he felt wrung out. Almost numb.

"Well, that sounds awful," Matthew said.

Tobias nodded. "It is. And I have no idea if things will ever get better."

"Can you bring Bloodbag in? I'd like to talk to him."

"Of course." Tobias stood, then walked down the hall to Bloodbag's room. He knocked on the door before poking his head in. It was dark, even for him, and it took a moment to spot Bloodbag huddled behind the chair in the corner.

"Bloodbag?" he said softly.

Bloodbag stirred, then gave a yelp of fright when he realized who was there. He scrambled out from behind the chair and rushed to kneel at Tobias's feet. "Bloodbag is sorry, Master."

"It's all right," Tobias said. "I have a friend here who would like to talk to you. He won't touch you or bite you. He just wants to talk. Come with me."

He led Bloodbag into his office and settled back into his chair. Bloodbag dropped to his knees next to Tobias, his eyes focused on the floor and his hands clasped in his lap. The stench of his anxiety filled the room.

"Hi, Bloodbag. I'm Matthew. I just want to chat. Is that all right?"

Bloodbag hesitated.

"You can talk to him," Tobias said quietly.

"Yes, sir," Bloodbag said.

"How old are you?"

"Thirty, sir."

Tobias raised an eyebrow. He had thought Bloodbag was a bit older, given the gray in his hair.

"How long have you been in vampire custody?"

"Ten years, sir."

"How many owners have you had?"

"Three. Bloodbag's first master only owned him for a couple months until he lost him to a friend in a card game. Bloodbag was with that master for the rest of the time until he was given to his current master a couple weeks ago."

Tobias gritted his teeth. Bloodbag had been kept and tortured for almost ten years by that sick bastard Phinney.

"Can you tell me a bit about your second master, the one you spent the most time with?"

"He . . . He was strict. He made sure Bloodbag learned to be good. He was thorough with his punishments."

"How did he punish you?" Matthew asked.

"His fists or the whip. Sometimes he would put the muzzle on Bloodbag. For the past year or so, Bloodbag spent most of the time chained."

"I see." Matthew paused. "Do you think you deserved those punishments?"

Bloodbag nodded emphatically. "Yes, sir. Bloodbag was bad and needed to be taught how to be good. Bloodbag is very grateful for his last master."

Tobias felt like he was going to be sick.

"Bloodbag, can you be honest with me?" Matthew asked.

"Yes, sir."

"Your current master has told you multiple times that he won't hurt you, yet you are still afraid. Can you tell me why that is?"

Bloodbag didn't respond. His face had gone pale, and Tobias could hear the pounding of his heart. The three of them sat in silence for one long minute.

"Bloodbag is weak and stupid," he said finally. "Bloodbag is afraid of punishment, even though Master says he won't punish Bloodbag. Bloodbag is afraid that Master will sell him to a bad place where Bloodbag will be killed. Bloodbag is afraid that Master will hurt Bloodbag. Bloodbag is scared because this is a new place, and he doesn't know the rules, and he doesn't know what Master wants from him, and he doesn't know what will earn him a punishment." Bloodbag took a deep breath. "Humans are always punished," he whispered. "Bloodbag doesn't believe Master."

Tobias's heart ached. Bloodbag had wrapped his arms around his stomach, and his tears dripped onto the floor.

"Thank you for your honesty," Matthew said, then flashed a look at Tobias. "It makes sense that you are scared, based on the past ten years. But you should know that your new master is kind, and he is merciful. He's a good friend of mine. He understands that this is all new for you, and he won't hurt you if you make a mistake. All he really wants is for you to be content."

"That's right," Tobias said. "I want you to feel safe here. I know I'm your master, but I would like to be your friend too. Do you think you can accept that?"

"Bloodbag can try, Master."

Well, at least that was a start.

13

—•—

Bloodbag didn't bother to wipe away the tears streaming down his face. Master and his friend knew he was weak. There was no point trying to hide it.

Bloodbag was being bad. Master didn't like him being scared, and he wanted to be a good pet for Master, but he was so afraid of being hurt. Bloodbag didn't believe the vampires when they said they wouldn't hurt him. He had never been around vampires who kept their promises. Master was obviously messing with his head.

Bloodbag was tired of always being scared, and Master seemed to know that. And so he'd offered him the one thing he wanted more than anything: a chance to be safe. It was cruel. So cruel. Bloodbag would rather be whipped than for Master to dangle hope and safety in front of his nose.

He hardly noticed Master's friend leaving the room with his vision so blurry with tears. Bloodbag went stiff when he saw Master's feet in front of him. He pressed his head to the floor.

"Bloodbag is sorry, Master. Bloodbag is sorry," he managed to choke out around his rattling sobs. He didn't know what Master really wanted, but it was clear that he didn't like it when Bloodbag cried.

A hand rested on his head, and he flinched. But Master didn't pull his hair or slap him. Instead, he gently stroked Bloodbag's hair. Bloodbag didn't know what to do, so he remained still. He knelt there, his sobs dying off as Master petted him.

"That's better," Master said once his sobs had stopped. "Can you sit up?"

Bloodbag straightened up with his eyes still focused on the floor.

"You've been really good, Bloodbag. I know you don't think you have been, but it's true. You try your best to please me, and that's what matters."

Bloodbag's heart skipped a beat. *Please him. That must be it.* Bloodbag's heart sank as he realized what Master wanted him to do. He should have seen it sooner.

Tears gathered in his eyes. That was one line his old master had never crossed. But this master was different.

"Bloodbag wants to please you, Master," he said, barely keeping his voice from breaking.

"I know," Master said softly. "I know." He sat down in a chair. "I need to feed."

Bloodbag climbed up into his lap, heart heavy. He pressed his forehead against Master's shoulder, giving him a clear space to bite his neck. The bright stab of fangs lit up his throat. Then it went numb, along with the rest of his body. He slumped against Master, his mind calming for the first time that night. He sat limp in Master's lap as Master drank.

Please Master, he thought before drifting off.

***

When Bloodbag awoke, he was alone in the chair. He sat up, a bit dizzy and with a sore neck. He got to his feet and walked into the hallway. A light flickered downstairs. Bloodbag glanced out one of the small windows to see pink tinging the horizon. Master would be going to bed soon.

Bloodbag quietly made his way to Master's bedroom. It was larger than his, with a big four-poster bed in the center. Bloodbag did his best to shut down his mind. He pulled his shirt over his head, then took off his trousers and underclothes. The air was cool against his bare skin, but he hardly noticed it as he neatly folded his clothes and set them on the floor.

He didn't know how Master wanted him—whether he wanted him kneeling on the floor or on the bed, or if he wanted him on all fours or bent over the bed.

Bloodbag got to his knees on the floor after a moment. He hoped Master would enjoy fucking him.

Bloodbag blinked back tears. He was ugly, he knew, with the scars that littered his back and neck and arms. But hopefully Master would be merciful and not mock him for that. He was just trying to be good, to please Master in any way he could. Master already had his blood, but it seemed he wanted the rest of his body as well.

Bloodbag's heart skipped a beat when he heard Master climbing the stairs. He had never been with a man before. Hopefully Master would teach him how to pleasure him properly.

Master entered the room and closed the door. He was facing away from Bloodbag as he approached the wardrobe, where he undressed. Bloodbag slammed his eyes shut as Master removed his trousers. It was too much. He let out a little sob.

"Bloodbag? What are you doing in here?" Master asked. His footsteps moved toward Bloodbag, then stopped dead.

"B-Bloodbag is here for you, Master."

Master took a couple more steps before he stood directly in front of Bloodbag, who reluctantly opened his eyes. Master was wearing a robe now.

"Master can take his pleasure as he wishes. Bloodbag will do anything Master wants."

"You . . . You think I want to rape you?"

"Bloodbag is just a human," Bloodbag said quietly. "It isn't rape if it's a human." He knew that. Humans were nothing.

"Get out," Master said through gritted teeth.

Bloodbag snapped his head up. Master looked furious. Bloodbag's heart dropped to his stomach.

"Now."

Bloodbag scrambled to his feet and raced for the door. His hand was shaking so much he could hardly turn the doorknob. Once he got the door open, he ran down the hall and into his room, slamming the door behind him. His legs gave out, and he collapsed to the floor.

He was confused. Master had said he wanted Bloodbag to please him. Bloodbag had thought that meant he wanted a sex slave, to use Bloodbag's body for his own pleasure. But as soon as Master had seen him, he had thrown him out. Was he too ugly?

A knock sounded on his door. Bloodbag got to his feet and opened it. Master stood on the other side. Bloodbag took a deep breath and surged forward, pressing a kiss against Master's lips. He wrapped his arms around Master's neck and kissed him like his life depended on it. Because it surely did. If Master wasn't satisfied, he would dispose of Bloodbag.

Bloodbag pushed his tongue into Master's mouth, desperately trying to make him happy. A moment later, Master was kissing him back. His tongue danced with Bloodbag's, and Bloodbag gave out a little whimper. He had never kissed anybody before, human or vampire. It was overwhelming.

He moved his hands to Master's robe and pushed it off his shoulders, then pressed his body against Master's. The vampire's skin was cool and soft. Bloodbag reached down between them to take Master's cock into his hand.

Master's fingers wrapped around Bloodbag's wrist.

"No," he said, his voice husky. "No. This is wrong." With his other hand, Master lifted Bloodbag's chin so that Bloodbag had to meet his eyes. "I know you don't really want this."

"But Bloodbag does. Bloodbag wants to make you happy."

Master sighed. He stroked Bloodbag's cheek with his thumb. "I know you do. But this isn't what you really want." Master stared pointedly down. Bloodbag followed his gaze to Master's semihard cock and then his own soft cock. "I'm not going to have sex with you, Bloodbag. Ever. Not because you're unattractive, but because I care about you, and I won't hurt you in that way."

"Bloodbag doesn't understand. Bloodbag thought Master wanted Bloodbag to please him."

"Not like this," Master said. "I want you to be happy. That's what will please me."

Bloodbag pondered that for a second. His hand rested on Master's chest. He closed his eyes. "Bloodbag is sorry. Bloodbag is stupid."

"No, Bloodbag, no," Master said gently. "You're not stupid. You are just trying to protect yourself. You were hurt for years, and it will take time for you to heal from that."

At those words, Bloodbag burst into tears. Master wrapped him in a hug, and Bloodbag buried his face against his shoulder.

"It's okay." Master rubbed Bloodbag's back. "It's okay."

"Bloodbag is too broken to ever get better. Bloodbag doesn't deserve Master's kindness."

"You're not broken. You learned how to survive, and now you just have to learn how to actually live again." Master led Bloodbag over to the bed. "Now get some rest."

Master left the room, quietly closing the door behind him. Then Bloodbag got onto the floor and curled up with his back against the wall. He needed something familiar when his entire life was changing around him.

14

—————— · ——————

Tobias clenched his teeth as he reached up to get some leather down from the shelf. He had only been back in the shop for a couple nights, and his entire body ached from the minimal activity he allowed himself to do.

"Master . . ."

Tobias closed his eyes and took a deep breath. He knew the human meant well, but sometimes he just wanted to suffer in peace.

"I'm fine, Bloodbag," he said shortly, wincing at how harsh his voice was.

Bloodbag didn't respond, and Tobias sighed. He sat down, setting to work on the boot that had been dropped off that evening. It was a simple repair. Before it would only have taken him a few minutes, but he had already tried three times and kept messing it up.

Tobias shifted his gaze from the boot in his hand to Bloodbag. He was in the same position he had been in for the last hour, kneeling on the wooden floor next to Tobias's chair. His hands were clasped in front of him, eyes focused on the floor—the picture of obedient submission.

Things had been . . . different since the incident. Tobias couldn't put his finger on exactly what had changed. Bloodbag was still scared of him, but that fear was now somewhat tempered.

"Bloodbag?"

He looked up at him.

"What do you know about the monks of Clea?"

Bloodbag's brow wrinkled. "Nothing, Master."

Tobias shook his head, trying to clear his thoughts. A bell rang above the door.

"Hello?" a familiar voice called.

Tobias smiled. "Back here." He looked up as Jonas walked into view.

He was short for a vampire, with black hair and skin as pale as snow. He also happened to be one of Tobias's few friends.

"Tobias!" Jonas said, reaching out to give him a hug.

Tobias gently put his hands out to stop him, skin stinging at the thought of a hug.

Jonas lowered his hands sheepishly. "Sorry, I forgot."

"No worries," Tobias said. "When did you get back from your trip?"

Jonas was a merchant, and he spent most of the year transporting goods between Torin and Lucia.

"Just a couple nights ago." He paused. "Are you all right? I heard about what happened."

Tobias shrugged. "Doing as well as can be expected. I won't be running into any other burning buildings anytime soon."

"No shit." Jonas gave an awkward chuckle as he shot a glance at Bloodbag. "So, what's with the blood bag?"

"I pulled him out of the fire, so his owner gave him to me."

"Really?" Jonas's eyebrows rose.

"Yes, really," Tobias said. "I've needed to feed a lot more often as I've been recovering."

"Huh." Jonas crossed his arms. "He doesn't look like much."

Tobias bristled. "He does the job," he said.

"I'm about to meet the boys to grab a drink at the pub. Want to come?"

Tobias's first instinct was to say no. He had a lot of work to do, and he wasn't sure if he would be able to keep up with his former drinking pace. But he hadn't had a good pint in forever.

"All right," he said. "Let's go."

Tobias took off his smock and set it over his chair before grabbing his and Bloodbag's coats from their hooks. He then attached the leash to Bloodbag's collar. Jonas led the way out of the shop, Tobias locking the door behind them.

Bloodbag didn't say a word as he trailed the two vampires down the street. The leash was loose in Tobias's hand, and if it weren't the law, he wouldn't have bothered with it. He knew Bloodbag wouldn't try to run.

The pub was crowded, the atmosphere rowdy. They pushed through the crowd to find the table that Aiden and Bruce had grabbed in the middle of the room.

"The hero fuckin' lives!" Bruce saluted Tobias with his mug.

"Aye, and the hero is fuckin' thirsty," Tobias said as he slid into a chair. Bloodbag knelt next to him, positioning himself so that he was basically under the table. Tobias put a reassuring hand on his head. Despite the reek of alcohol and unwashed bodies, he could smell Bloodbag's fear.

The drinks kept coming. Tobias was surprised at how well he was able to keep up. His belly and cheeks were warm, and he laughed as they chatted and joked.

"How are you liking having your own human?" Aiden asked. It was late, the pub calmer. Tobias laughed.

"The blood is great. The human is the problem." Somewhere deep inside, he winced at the words, but he ignored that feeling. "He's always scared, he begs me not to hurt him, he asks to be punished. I don't know what he wants." Tobias took a sip of his beer before slamming it onto the table. "His old master was going to get rid of him, and I see why. He really is a handful." The feeling that he should quit talking was growing, but Tobias was on a roll now, all of the frustrations of the past weeks coming forward. "Sometimes I have half a mind to wash my hands of him."

"Why don't you? He seems like more trouble than he's worth."

Tobias snorted. "I don't think anyone would take him."

"You could try a blood butcher."

"No. Even though the little fucker gets on my last nerve, he doesn't deserve that."

"Well, why not?"

"Because he'll be killed at a blood butcher," Tobias said.

"Yeah, that's kinda the point." They rolled their eyes.

"And don't you think that's wrong? To send humans to their deaths as soon as they become a bit of trouble?" Tobias drained the rest of his mug in one gulp.

They shrugged. "They're just humans."

"What do you mean, they're just humans?" Tobias asked, anger coiling.

"They're animals. Expendable. Good for their blood and little else."

"That seems to be what you've been saying all night, Tobias," Jonas said.

"N-no, that's not what I meant."

The conversation moved on, and everyone was laughing. Just then, Tobias remembered he had a companion under the table. He glanced down to see Bloodbag completely still, tears streaming down his face. His hands shook, and utter terror radiated off of him.

"Ah, shit," Tobias muttered. "I've got to go," he said more loudly, abruptly getting to his feet. He gave a short tug on the leash, and Bloodbag followed him, wiping the snot from his nose with his sleeve.

"Aw, where ya goin'?" Bruce asked.

"I have to get Bloodbag home," Tobias said.

"Fuckin' humans," Jonas said.

But Tobias was already halfway out the door. The street was quiet, the sky just starting to take on the pale gray of dawn.

"I'm sorry, Bloodbag. I shouldn't have said those things."

Bloodbag didn't respond, his gaze fixed on the ground.

"Bloodbag, look at me," Tobias said, tilting Bloodbag's chin up.

"You hate me," Bloodbag said. "It's my fault that you were hurt, and I'm nothing but a burden to you."

"No, Bloodbag. That's not true."

"Can we go home, Master?" Bloodbag whispered.

Tobias deflated. "Yeah, let's go home."

The walk back was silent, guilt eating at Tobias's stomach. Gods, why had he said all those awful things? He cared about Bloodbag, truly. It was just that he had been so frustrated.

A weight settled on Tobias's shoulders. How could he—someone planning on joining the monks of Clea and dedicating his life to humans—have been so cruel to one? Yes, he'd been drunk, but that wasn't an excuse. He had sinned against the goddess.

15

They climbed the steps to the front door. Bloodbag took off his shoes and coat. Tobias reached out to undo his collar, and Bloodbag just stared at the floor. Once the collar was off, Bloodbag headed toward his room without a word.

Tobias ran a hand through his hair. He'd fucked up. He winced when his stomach growled. He needed to feed after all that alcohol, but he couldn't bring himself to hurt Bloodbag like that, to rub it in his face that he was just a meal.

Tobias headed for the kitchen. He would bring Bloodbag a plate with some of his favorite foods. He got out the strawberries, the sharp cheddar that smelled like death but Bloodbag seemed to love, the jerky, and the sweet bread. Satisfied, he headed to Bloodbag's room.

He knocked on the door. "Bloodbag? I have something for you." No response. Tobias stood there a moment. Maybe Bloodbag was asleep. He knocked louder. "Bloodbag?" Still no response. He bit his lip. Bloodbag wasn't such a heavy sleeper that he wouldn't wake up at a loud knock.

"I'm coming in." Tobias opened the door. Bloodbag was lying face down on the bed. Tobias set the tray on the chair to shake Bloodbag's shoulder. He didn't respond. "Bloodbag?" Tobias rolled him onto his back. His face was pale, his eyes closed. "Bloodbag!"

Tobias put a hand on his cheek, but he didn't respond. He wasn't asleep; he was unconscious. Panic gripped Tobias's throat.

"Shit, fuck, fuck." Tobias ran his hands through his hair. He searched wildly around the room. There wasn't anything that Bloodbag could have gotten into, anything poisonous. His mind raced back to the pub. Had Bloodbag eaten or drank anything there? No, Tobias was almost certain he hadn't.

He looked down at his human. He was breathing, his heart rate steady, but he wouldn't wake up. Tobias grabbed the glass of water and splashed it in Bloodbag's face. Nothing.

He raced out of the room. He had a book on humans, one he'd gotten recently. He flipped to the section on illness. Nowhere was a mention of a human who wouldn't wake up. He threw the book down in frustration and walked back to Bloodbag's room, the anxiety making it hard to breathe.

As he walked in, Bloodbag opened his eyes. Tobias almost cried in relief.

"You're awake! I was so worried." He clasped Bloodbag's hand in his own. But Bloodbag didn't respond. His gaze was glassy, and perspiration coated his face. "Can you hear me?"

Tobias swallowed the bile in his throat when Bloodbag didn't move. "Okay, okay. I'll help you. I'll take you to the temple. They'll know what to do." It was the spring equinox festival and all the veterinarians would be closed. Tobias quickly pulled on his shoes and coat.

He wrapped a blanket around Bloodbag and picked him up so he was cradled in his arms. Then he sprinted out the door.

***

Tobias's feet flew over the cobblestones. The streets were packed with revelers, and they shot Tobias dirty looks as he pushed past them. It was only a twenty-minute walk to the temple on a regular night, and Tobias prayed he would get there in time. He didn't know what was happening to Bloodbag, but he would never forgive himself if Bloodbag died thinking Tobias hated him.

"Excuse me, excuse me!" Tobias pushed through the crowd. Bloodbag whimpered in his arms. Why were all these people in his way?

"And I tell you, my brothers and sisters! Lebne will be coming soon to free us from our hunger! And when he does, he will expect us to smite his sister, that evil demoness, Clea. Her time is over, and it is time for the true god to rise!"

Cheers filled the streets as the blood drained from Tobias's face.

No. How could all these people be buying this?

"Tonight, heretics are worshipping this false goddess. Let us show them who the true god is!"

The crowd surged forward, and Tobias stumbled. He clutched Bloodbag tight to his chest as they were swept up in the crowd. People pushed him from behind, and he had no choice but to keep up with those in front of him. Angry yells filled the air. Tobias jolted at the sounds of screams. The two groups were clashing.

He was knocked to his knees, and Bloodbag fell out of his arms. "Bloodbag!"

He struggled to get to his feet, but once he had, he'd already lost Bloodbag in the crowd. "Bloodbag!" Tobias pushed through the angry people. "Bloodbag!" His voice broke, and his heart pounded right out of his chest.

Bloodbag was gone.

***

"Please, have you seen a human?" Tobias asked the man next to him.

"No," the man replied, distracted.

Tobias must have asked a dozen people, but every answer was the same. No one had seen Bloodbag. His mind raced through every possible scenario: Bloodbag trampled to death, his body broken under the weight of the crowd's frenzy; Bloodbag bitten and bleeding, his lifeless body slumped in an alley; or worse, Bloodbag taken to one of the blood butchers, where he would be drugged and beaten and bled until he died.

Tobias managed to stumble out of the crowd. He braced his hands against a cool brick wall, sweat dripping down his body. He had to find him. He had to.

A scream split the air. Tobias whipped his head around to see flames shooting into the night.

As if tonight couldn't get any worse, an overwhelming need to run hit him. The flames cast an orange glow over the city, and terror engulfed him. Tobias could feel the heat on his skin, the burning of his flesh. He could smell it. He shrank back against the building.

"Help me, Goddess," he pleaded. "Please help me." He couldn't breathe. He sank to the ground as his limbs shook. Tobias wrapped his hand around his pendant, squeezing it so hard that the sunrays dug into his skin. He took a breath.

Then he got to his feet. He was terrified, but Bloodbag needed him. He knew what he needed to do. "Goddess, give me strength." With a final steadying breath, he pushed off the wall and headed back into the streets.

16

Tobias raced down the street. The yells of the crowd echoed in his ears, but his world had narrowed to a single objective: find Bloodbag. He skidded to a stop as the smell of blood hit his nose. He whipped his head to the right to a dark narrow alley.

Tobias stalked into the alley, clenching and unclenching his fists. Whatever was down there, he was going to be ready.

"Please, sir. Please have mercy." The meager voice echoed down the alley.

Tobias's stomach dropped. It was Bloodbag.

"Shut up, bitch." A slap rang out, followed by a string of laughs.

Tobias turned a corner to see Bloodbag pinned against the brick wall, blood dripping down his face. Five vampires surrounded him.

Tobias stayed in the shadows as he considered his options. He couldn't take on five men. Even in his best shape, he would almost certainly be beaten to a pulp. Weakened as he was from lack of blood, he had no chance.

Bloodbag cried out as one of the bastards stabbed his fangs into the side of his neck. Tobias gritted his teeth and stepped forward.

"Leave him alone!" he shouted.

The four unoccupied vampires turned toward him.

"Fuck off," one of them spit.

"That's my human you're abusing," he said. "Let him go."

"We ain't abusing the blood bag. We're just showing him a good time." His eyes narrowed. "You better not be one of those human fuckers."

Tobias clenched his fists so hard he was sure he was ripping holes in his palms. "Let. Him. Go."

"I think we have to teach this fucker some respect."

Two of the vampires rushed Tobias. He managed to dodge the first blow, but the second one caught him in the stomach. Tobias gasped as the air was driven from his lungs. Then he was on the ground, curling in on himself to defend against the vicious kicks.

"Master!"

Tobias blinked his eyes open. He was lying on the ground, his face resting in a warm puddle. A puddle of his own blood. He groaned as he pushed himself up to his hands and knees. The vampires shared a laugh, patting each other on the back. Bloodbag was curled up against the wall, his hands wrapped around his stomach. He looked at Tobias with wide eyes.

Tobias's hand hit something sharp. He looked down to see shards of broken glass. He grabbed the two biggest pieces, testing the weight in his hands. His head was spinning, and everything hurt, but he would save Bloodbag.

Tobias roared as he ran at the vampires. He flailed around with the glass, not knowing what he was doing. Whatever it was, it worked.

The vampires ran off, and Tobias fell to his knees next to Bloodbag. He wrapped his arms around him.

"You're safe now. You're safe."

Bloodbag sobbed as Tobias rubbed his back. "I-I was so scared. I woke up on the ground, and there were people screaming, and then those vampires dragged me into the alley, and—"

"I'm sorry." Tobias planted a gentle kiss on his forehead. "I'm so sorry." He stood up shakily, helping Bloodbag stand as well. "Let's get you to the temple."

Bloodbag stood for only a moment before his knees gave way. Tobias caught him before he fell to the ground.

"I'm sorry, Master. I don't think I can walk."

"That's okay. I'll carry you." Tobias scooped Bloodbag up into his arms.

Bloodbag pressed his face against Tobias's chest. "I don't feel good."

"I know. We're going to the temple, all right? The monks there should know what to do."

Tobias strode out of the alley. He didn't like how Bloodbag looked. His face was pale, and his body and clothes were coated in blood from the abuse he'd suffered. He had been ill to begin with, and add on top of that substantial blood loss . . . Well, Tobias would be relieved once they reached the temple.

The sounds of clashing groups still echoed through the city. When Tobias turned the corner onto the final street, there was a mob. He cursed. Members of the city militia surrounded the temple. They were trying to maintain order but seemed to be failing.

"People of Cesvic!" A man climbed the steps of the temple. His blue robes marked him as a priest of Lebne. "You are faithful to our god, and he sees this and smiles upon it. But anger toward his sister is unacceptable. The twin deities work in tandem, balancing each other. We cannot have one without the other."

"We're hungry!" someone called. "We're hungry, and Clea does nothing to satiate our thirst."

Murmurs of agreement rippled through the crowd.

The priest put up his hands in a calming gesture. "I understand your pain. This is but a test. Our gods need us to work together to find a solution, not fight amongst ourselves. Attacking those faithful to the goddess will not ease your thirst."

"Then what will?"

"There is a new shipment of humans set to arrive within the week. Over a hundred of them. I have coordinated with the traders to make sure the blood will be distributed fairly across the city, starting with those most in need."

A cheer rang out.

"This ordeal will be over soon, my friends," the priest said. "Now please go back to your homes. The night is almost over. Spend it in prayer. By the full moon, the humans will be here, and you will no longer be hungry."

Gradually, the crowd dispersed. Once it was clear, Tobias walked to the steps of the temple. Mora was there talking to the priest. Tobias caught her gaze, and her eyes widened when she saw Bloodbag in his arms.

"Excuse me," she told the priest. He gave her a slight bow as she approached Tobias. "What happened?"

"He was attacked," Tobias said, his voice breaking. "He lost a lot of blood."

"Come with me." She led them into the temple and locked the door behind her.

17

—·—

"Tell me everything," Mora said as she opened the door to what appeared to be an infirmary. She gestured for Tobias to lay Bloodbag on one of the beds.

Tobias's hands shook as he smoothed back Bloodbag's hair. "Earlier this evening, I found him unconscious in his room. I tried everything, but he wouldn't wake up. I didn't know what to do, so I decided to come here for help. On the way, we got swept up in the crowd. I dropped him, and we were separated." Tobias choked on the word. "It was an accident."

"Of course." Mora placed a soothing hand on his arm. "Then what happened?"

"I searched for probably half an hour before I smelled the blood. Five vampires had dragged him into an alley and were feeding on him. He had woken up sometime before I found him. He was terrified." Tobias swallowed past the lump in his throat. "I managed to get him away from them, but he had already been fed on. I have no idea how much blood he lost. He couldn't stand, much less walk."

Mora nodded. "I'll get Benedict to prepare a tonic. Meanwhile, the first order of business is to clean and bandage the wounds. I'll be right back." She left the room, moving quickly.

"Master?" Bloodbag whispered.

Tobias clasped Bloodbag's hand between both of his own. "Yes, I'm here."

"What's happening?"

"We're at the Temple of Clea," Tobias said. "The monks here are skilled in healing humans. They're going to help you."

Bloodbag nodded.

Mora returned with a bowl and some bandages.

"My name is Mora," she said as she sat down next to Bloodbag. "I'm here to help. I need to clean and bandage your wounds. I'll be gentle, I promise."

"Yes, ma'am," Bloodbag said.

"I'm going to need you to take off your shirt."

Bloodbag complied. Tobias gasped when he saw the angry bruises covering his torso. Mora shot him a meaningful look. Tobias clamped his mouth shut as rage filled him. How dare they do this to him?

The bite marks were mostly on his neck, though one was right above his collarbone on the left side, and another was squarely on his right forearm. Bloodbag whimpered as Mora touched the bite on his arm.

"I'm sorry. I know it hurts," she said. "I would give you venom, but Tobias said you were unconscious earlier, and the venom could be dangerous. I'll be quick."

Bloodbag didn't respond, but he made a visible effort to relax his muscles.

Mora dabbed at the wound, then wrapped a clean white bandage around it before moving on to the other ones.

As she was finishing up, another monk with white hair and a deeply lined face entered the room with a tray in hands. He set the tray on a table and handed a bowl to Mora. "This should help restore his strength."

Bloodbag drained the entire bowl. When he was finished, he leaned back on the bed. His heavy eyelids drooped.

"Rest," Mora said. "You're safe here."

Bloodbag's breathing slowly evened out. Tobias sighed in relief when he was finally asleep.

"Come, Tobias," Mora said. "There's much to discuss."

Tobias followed Mora out of the infirmary and into a large common room. He stopped in his tracks when he saw at least a dozen humans staring at him. His cheeks heated from the attention.

Mora led him into an office. Benedict was already there, sitting in a chair by a fireplace.

"Please sit."

Tobias settled into the indicated chair.

"My name is Benedict, and I am in charge of the temple, at least for the time being. I'll be retiring sometime in the next couple years, and Mora will take over then. She told me you are considering joining the Order."

Tobias sucked in a breath. It was one thing to think about it, but to actually tell the monks that he wanted to join them, to be serious about it . . .

Tobias closed his eyes for a moment. When he opened them, he was sure.

"Yes, I would like to join the Order."

Benedict nodded. "We would be happy to have you. Right now, there are four monks here and fourteen humans."

"What is the process?"

"It usually takes three years to become a full monk. The first year, you will be considered an acolyte. You will spend much of your time learning the scriptures and prayers and assisting with various everyday tasks. The next year, you will be allowed to help with services. Once we are satisfied with your performance, you will go through the final test. It is a month-long fast, during which you will not feed at all. At the end of the fast, you will swear your loyalty to every human in our care. Only then will you be allowed to feed and join the Order."

Tobias's mouth went dry at the idea of not feeding for an entire month.

"It is not for the faint of heart," Benedict said. "Our priority is the safety of our humans. The fast is meant to ensure that your loyalty to the goddess—and the humans in our care—is stronger than your base desires. Here at the temple, we never feed from our humans without their permission and never ask to feed except in an emergency. They offer their blood to us of their own free will, and we accept their gift."

"I understand." Tobias licked his lips. "I would like to bring my human. The one in the infirmary right now."

"I figured as much. Once you enter into the temple, you will sign a transfer of ownership. This will mark him legally as the property of the goddess, with the temple acting as her representative. This is irreversible. Once he belongs to her, you can never take him back as your personal property."

"Are the humans here . . . happy?"

Benedict gave him a small smile. "You can ask them that for yourself."

— · —

Epilogue

Finally. It had been three long years, but today, Tobias would finally be fully initiated as a monk of Clea. He fastened the belt around his waist with shaky hands. It had been a month since his last meal. It had been painful, but it was almost over.

Tobias opened the door and stepped out of his small room. His initiation was to take place in the main temple at sunrise. As Clea rose to greet the world, he would kneel before each human at the temple, kissing their wrists as he swore his devotion to each of them.

Everybody was gathered in the temple. Candles sparkled from every ledge, bathing the space in low orange light.

Benedict said, "Today we welcome a new brother to our order: Tobias. He has shown himself to be a true disciple of the goddess over his years of training."

Tobias knelt before the first human, gingerly taking their wrists. He pressed a kiss against one, then the other, feeling their blood pulsing underneath the thin skin. The temptation to sink his fangs in and drink his fill was strong, but he pushed it down.

Finally, the last human stood before him. Bloodbag. Tobias pressed a kiss to his left wrist, then his right.

"Welcome, Brother Tobias," Benedict said.

A cheer went up, and a smile split Tobias's face. He had done it. He was about to get to his feet when Bloodbag knelt before him.

"Please, Tobias, feed," he said softly.

"Thank you," Tobias whispered. He pressed a kiss to both sides of his neck. "Thank you for the gift of the blood that flows through your veins." He kissed both wrists again. "May I be a worthy vessel." Then he bit down gently on the side of his neck. Bloodbag went limp as the venom hit, but Tobias didn't let him fall. He wrapped Bloodbag in his arms as the hot savory blood reached his tongue. Tears ran down his cheeks as he drank. He was so hungry.

When his stomach could hold no more, he pulled back and lapped at the puncture wounds. The bleeding slowed until it finally stopped.

"Thank you, Bloodbag," Tobias whispered.

Bloodbag gave him a sleepy smile. "You're welcome. Can you take me back to my room?"

Tobias nodded, scooping Bloodbag up in his arms. He held him close as he carried him back into the rectory. He laid him down on his bed and wrapped a blanket around him.

"Tobias?" Bloodbag licked his lips. "Before I became Bloodbag, I had a name."

Tobias froze. He had asked once what Bloodbag's real name was, but he hadn't answered. "Yes?" he said carefully.

"I . . . I think I want to start using it again."

Tobias smiled. "That sounds like a great idea."

"My name was—or is, I guess—Ira."

Tobias smelled a note of fear on him, and his heart ached. It had surely been beaten into Ira that he wasn't allowed to have a real name.

Tobias gently took his hand. "That's a wonderful name. It's very nice to meet you, Ira."

Ira smiled at him. "It's very nice to meet you too."

With that, Ira closed his eyes and drifted to sleep.

Tobias quietly shut the door and headed downstairs. Now that he was a full monk, he had duties to attend to. Benedict had assigned him to lead the morning prayers.

Tobias stepped back into the temple, and the scent of incense hit him. He breathed in. He was home.

Light streamed through the stained glass windows, flooding the temple with warmth. Tobias joined Mora in front of the altar. She handed him the brazier with incense. He bowed to the statue of Clea, then made his way around the round altar. The incense curled up into the air.

"Goddess of the sun," he began. "Goddess of the day. Goddess of the morning, of the rising and the setting. Goddess of fire, of warmth, of comfort. Goddess of humans and of blood. We thank you for the new day, for your many wonderful gifts. May you look upon your servants with kindness."

AN EXCERPT FROM CRY OF FANGS

Aldon had never drank directly from the vein before. That changed, as it did for all vampire children, on his thirteenth birthday.

Aldon stood in front of his father, stomach in knots.

"Today, you transition from boy to man. Don't you dare disappoint me."

"Yes sir," Aldon said. As if he had ever done anything that *hadn't* disappointed his father. His first feeding was to take place at his grandparents' house just outside the city. It was to be a grand event; all his aunts and uncles and cousins would be there to see him cross the threshold to adulthood.

Aldon had seen humans from a distance before, but he'd never actually touched one. His family couldn't afford their own human. Instead, they bought their blood from the local blood butcher. The idea of having to bite a human, to have its flesh in his mouth, made him shiver.

He had friends who'd already gone through their first feedings, and they enjoyed making him squirm with their descriptions—how horribly warm human skin was, the awful stench of fear, the way their flesh ripped apart under vampire fangs. After one particularly . . . descriptive story, Aldon had retreated behind a tree in the schoolyard to be sick.

The carriage ride wasn't long. Aldon felt ill by the time they arrived.

"Welcome, my sweet boy!" His grandmother wrapped him in a big hug, and he squeezed her back.

His grandfather clapped him on the back. "Today's a big day, isn't it, sport?"

Aldon licked his lips. "It is. Have to admit, I'm kinda nervous."

"No reason to be nervous at all. Humans don't bite!" Aldon's grandfather laughed at his own joke, clapping Aldon on the back again and leading him inside.

Feeding was a private affair, so Aldon entered the dark room alone. His eyes alighted on the figure huddled on the floor—his human for the night. Aldon gulped.

He timidly made his way across the stone floor. He couldn't make out much of the human; they were curled in a fetal position, and their back was turned to him. As he got closer, he detected a smell in the air. It wasn't exactly what his friends had described. It wasn't pungent and sour. It was more . . . sad.

Aldon stood next to the human. It was a male, curled up with his knees pulled to his chest. He was naked except for a ragged pair of brown trousers. This close, Aldon could see the bruises all over his skin—yellows and greens and purples. He could also see the scars. They were everywhere, all down his neck, his arms, even his chest. Aldon's mouth went dry. The humans still hadn't moved to acknowledge Aldon's presence.

This was wrong. Aldon knew it in his bones. Humans were prey—they were an inferior species—but that didn't mean they should be abused.

Aldon stepped around the human, then sat down, crossing his legs. The human opened his eyes, staring at Aldon with resignation.

"Um, I'm Aldon. I don't really know what to do. This is my first time feeding from a human . . ."

Stupid. He was just stupid. Nobody talked to their meals.

A quiet chuckle. "No vampire has ever introduced themselves before feeding before."

Aldon jumped a little. He hadn't expected the human to respond.

"Do you have a name?" Aldon asked.

The human pushed himself up into a seated position. "Nobody has ever asked me that either. Usually, I'm just called 745, but my name is Julian."

"It's a pleasure to meet you, Julian," Aldon said. He had been taught to be polite to his elders, and even though Julian was human, he was clearly older than him.

"Sorry to say the feeling isn't mutual. If I were going to survive the night, I'd be more sociable. You seem like a nice kid."

Aldon's eyes went wide. "What? What do you mean? I'm not going to drain you."

Julian gave Aldon a sad smile. "Your family will. The boss has decided that I've reached the end of my usefulness. Gotten too ugly. He gave your kin a special deal. They'll drain me before I make it to another sunrise." He said all this matter-of-factly, and it sent chills down Aldon's spine.

"I'm sorry. I didn't know."

Julian gave a little shrug, the light catching on his scarred shoulders. "It is what it is."

"Is there anything I can do? To make you more comfortable?"

Julian looked at Aldon with raised brows, and his mouth parted. His bottom lip quivered. Then he put his head in his hands and started to sob—great heaving sobs that shook his whole body. Aldon scooted closer and wrapped his arms around the human. Julian stiffened, then relaxed into Aldon's embrace. He was bigger than Aldon but extremely thin. And he was warm, just like Aldon's friends had said. But the warmth wasn't revolting like Aldon had expected. It was actually rather comforting. They sat like that for a while, the scarred human man crying in the arms of the scared vampire boy.

***

Aldon emerged from the room, mouth bloody, his family cheering. He gave a weak smile, then excused himself to wash up. He went to the bathroom and shut the door behind him. His stomach heaved, and he vomited up all the blood he'd just drank, then sank down with his back against the closed door as tears ran down his face.

Soon came a pounding on the door.

"Young man, you were just supposed to feed, not tear its throat out! You're lucky we already paid for it in full . . ." The anger in his father's voice mixed with pride.

Aldon ignored him, his mind trapped by Julian's last whispered words: *Thank you.*

ACKNOWLEDGEMENTS

This small but mighty book would never had made it to see the light of day without the support of many, many people. First off, I would like to thank my family for encouraging me to keep writing when I felt like giving up. Mom, Dad, and Nicki, you guys are truly the best. I love you!

I also would like to thank Chelsea and Natalia from Enchanted Ink Publishing for their editorial expertise. Any errors that remain are entirely my responsibility.

Thank you to all of the readers who found OVAM online and fell in love with my angsty vampire boys. I have read every single comment and tag, and every one makes me the happiest dang author in the whole dang world. A special shout out to Z, Mill, Mouse, and Mars, for being some of my biggest supporters. And an extra special shout out to Red, whose one comment inspired me to explore Tobias and Ira's backstory.

Finally, I want to thank you, dear reader, for spending some time with me and my vampires. I hope you enjoyed the journey. If you did, please consider leaving a review for this book. As an indie author, reviews help me out a lot! Now good night, sleep tight, and don't let the vampires bite.

ABOUT THE AUTHOR

Kailey Alessi is the founder and editor-in-chief of the Whumpy Printing Press, a publishing company whose mission is to publish the work of the whump community. Kailey has lived in Michigan, Kentucky, Idaho, and Florida (but she's a midwestern girl at heart). She is an archaeologist by day, and by night she writes all sorts of dark fiction.

www.ingramcontent.com/pod-product-compliance
Lightning Source LLC
Chambersburg PA
CBHW050857150626
46549CB00013B/2901